Advance Praise for *Things That Cause Inappropriate Happiness*

We humans: what an endless braid of tender, joyful, painful, loving emotional pas de deux we live. In these stories, Danila Botha examines the complex knotting and unknotting of these contemporary relationships with vivid insight, deep compassion, and unflinching incision. They are virtuoso variations about what makes us human, what makes us—and our stories—irresistible, moving and compelling.

—Gary Barwin, award-winning author of *Yiddish for Pirates*, *Nothing the Same, Everything Haunted*, and co-author of *duck eats yeast, quacks, explodes; man loses eye*.

This book is pure, raw power. Like Botha's other work, the stories in *Things That Cause Inappropriate Happiness* push against every boundary, offering unsettling glimpses into the wars women wage on their bodies, the messiness of finding and losing love, the self-sabotaging patterns that both propel and hold back. Botha is a master of balance, offering switchbacks between the pristine beauty of actual happiness paired with deep, unapologetic rage rooted in larger contexts like the patriarchy and historical genocides. Each story feels so real—the clear and authentic character voices often hold the power to reveal the exact essence of a character, sometimes in a single sentence. Though these stories capture a wide range of geographies and experiences, they always reflect on important, universal questions—where are the boundaries of forgiveness? Where is the line between two much and not enough?

—Leesa Dean, author of *Waiting for the Cyclone* and *Filling Station*

Powerful and searing glimpses into people's most intimate emotions. Danila Botha's writing makes the reader stop cold, sit up and listen. She expertly finds deceptively quiet moments in her characters' lives, that by the end of her stories, reveal themselves to be more pivotal than we first realized. The characters in this collection will stay with me for a long time. An exquisite book.

—Sidura Ludwig, author of the Dan… Gleed Award winning collection *You Are Not What We Expec…*

Incredibly deep and powerful … [the stories] feel like John Cheever's "Reunion," using what's said and what's not said to give us a novel's worth of story … It's a brilliant display of technical skill and a satisfying read, and [it] greatly impresses me.

—JJ Dupuis, author of the *Creature X Mystery* series

This sparkling collection documents the inner lives of girls and women with vivid emotion and delicious attitude. Botha's brilliant stories demand to be chewed on, mulled over, and talked about. Casting off the expectations of traditional style, they offer readers the comfort of generational wisdom and a clear-eyed view of our tumultuous present.

—Carleigh Baker, award-winning author of *Bad Endings*, *Mudlarkers* and *Last Woman*

In these deft short stories, Danila Botha explores the desires of a cast of young, urban artists driven to escape their circumstances, from trendy Shakshuka bars to reality matchmaking shows to the horrors of the Holocaust. With fine prose and tender insight, Botha has written an indelible collection.

—Kathy Friedman, author of *All the Shining People*

Praise for Danila Botha's previous books

For All the Men (and Some of the Women) I've Known

Everyone in this book is alive. Painfully, nervously, ardently. This collection (like Chekhov by way of Kathy Acker but utterly original) is truthful and dreamy, tough and tremulous; sad and aching, seductively, with hope.

—Lynn Crosbie, author of *Where Did You Sleep Last Night*

For All the Men and Some of the Women I've Known is unlike anything I have ever read before. Unflinchingly honest in its examination of love in all its joyful, messy, agonizing, spectacularly beautiful glory, these stories seem to vibrate on their own emotional frequency. Danila Botha writes with a heartbreaking rawness and intensity that will continue to haunt you long after you've turned the final page.

—Amy Jones, author of *We're All In This Together*

These stories are written in a gutsy, head-on, colloquial style about love, sex and mis-connection among the urban 20-somethings she knows so well. Her characters are all compulsively themselves, driven, probably always, to make a mess of things, but vulnerable, full of desire, and often touchingly witty.

—Douglas Glover, author of *Elle*

This collection might be Botha's most triumphant work to date … *For All The Men* … has Botha delivering smart prose that seamlessly balances humour, disappointment and dysfunction … In addition to sharp and perceptive characterization, Botha's writing is perfectly paced. The reader repeatedly discovers moments in which everything seems to fall together: a character pulls you in, a beautiful scene is set, and before you know it, devastation unfolds … But Botha is consistently sympathetic to her characters' experiences … Botha is an incredibly fresh voice in Canadian literature, and this visceral and remarkable collection feels like it's only setting the stage for much more to come.

—*Quill and Quire Magazine* (Starred Review)

Like a series of orchestral variations whose loops and iterations are made vital by the steady introduction of new elements … These are stories full of people who disappoint, or are disappointed, yet they rarely end on a note of despair, which in today's Tinder-enabled relationship landscape seems almost like an act of subversion. She has a fine talent too, for putting emphasis in unexpected places … This unexpectedness can extend to Botha's turns of phrase, which offers a wry counterpoint to her project as a whole.

—*The Toronto Star*

Power dynamics pervade Danila Botha's sophomore collection, which focuses on the romantic travails of a group of urban twenty somethings falling into and out of love, lust and friendship … Botha's characters freely indulge in sex and drugs and copious amounts of alcohol in their quest to find succour or peace, though it becomes readily apparent that what they are most intent on discovering—and what proves most elusive—is some sort of authentic connection with another human being … The author is undeniably familiar with modern urban ennui, and the stories in her collection have an admirable directness and grit … Botha is clear-eyed in illustrating the ways her protagonists' devotion

to their vision of romantic purity is either subverted or results in the unintended consequence of alienating the very object of their longing.
—*The Globe and Mail*

Too Much on the Inside

Danila Botha's new novel is a kind of bouquet—a vase full of life snippets from Toronto's late-night world. Sweet and sharp, musky and startling, and full of yearning, the lives of these recent arrivals mingle together to create a vivid sense experience. *Too Much On The Inside* is an easy read in the best sense of the word: pacy, deftly plotted, hugely enjoyable.
—Richard Scrimger, *Mystical Rose*

Danila Botha's debut novel tells the extraordinary story of four individuals whose lives intersect in Toronto's Parkdale neighbourhood. The narrative, which is constructed in alternating first-person voices, reveals a deep understanding of human nature … By the novel's end … Botha makes clear [that love is] the only thing that can save these characters.
—*Quill and Quire Magazine*

Danila Botha, whose first book drew praise for its compassion and urgency, brings similar sentiments to her interwoven portrayals of four new Torontonians of diverse origin (South Africa, Brazil, Israel and Nova Scotia) drawn to the openness and opportunities they sense Queen Street West might offer them … There is an admirable freshness and enthusiasm in Botha's writing, qualities that do not inhibit her ability to describe dark and even violent events.
—Amy Lavender-Harris, the *Literary Review of Canada*

Too Much On The Inside is a multi-narrated elegy to Toronto's Queen West neighbourhood that is both candid and wise.
—Marissa Stapley, *The Toronto Star*

"Aptly set in the heart of Toronto's mecca for self-expression, Queen St. West … Danila Botha's greatest achievement lies in the power of her highly authentic portrayal of these disparate voices … Recently landed immigrants, and indeed anyone who has experienced the simultaneous elation and dread that accompanies embarking on a new relationship, will see themselves here. *Too Much on the Inside* will surprise you with its insights and comfort you with its wide appeal.

—*Broken Pencil Magazine*

An earthy portrait of love, loss, and confronting the past set in Toronto's Queen St. West, Danila Botha's first novel is incredibly moving, gritty, and authentic … *Too Much on the Inside* is an exploration of four fascinatingly dissimilar characters whose lives intersect and influence each other irrevocably. The novel reminds me of the fugal interlacing of P.T. Anderson's *Magnolia* and the down-to-earth sincerity of J.K. Rowling's A *Casual Vacancy* … Botha's writing is masterful—deceptively simple, with an astonishing attention to detail that creates a multi-coloured fabric of distinct locales and personalities.

—Mike Fan, *The Book Shelf*, Guelph

[*Too Much on the Inside*] is full of energy, enthusiasm, and compassion … Danila seems to have bottled youth in this book, with its four narrators, Nicki, Dez, Lukas, and Marlize, all facing Toronto as relative newcomers trying to deal with their prior lives … these are powerful voices, fizzing and competing to be heard.

—Alix Hawley

[An] insightful and compassionately written novel about the lives of four twenty-somethings who are recent arrivals to Toronto … This is very much a Toronto (and a love letter to Queen West) story seen through the eyes of those not born here … The author did a terrific job exploring the aftermath of what it's like to grow up in contexts of violence, and how each character must ask themselves how they now can try to be good people.

—Farzana Doctor

Got No Secrets

These stories grab you by the throat and don't let go, bearing witness to lives in which self- destruction and hope are like symbionts, each feeding the other.

—Nino Ricci

Danila Botha's stories are both intriguing and disturbing. Dealing in subjects like abuse, rape and addiction, she manages never to alienate the reader. Her voice becomes particularly unique in the way she combines the South African and Canadian experience. A new writer with great promise.

—Melinda Ferguson

Danila Botha is an emerging literary lioness on Canada's literary landscape ... *Got No Secrets* packs an emotional wallop ... powerful and poignant ... an honest and freshly forthright debut that is filled with the headaches and heartburns of youth gone awry.

—*The Chronicle Herald*, Halifax

In the tradition of Canadian women authors like Zoe Whittall and Heather O'Neill, these short stories ... thrust you into the characters' minds with equal parts sympathy and self-awareness ... The visceral prose most effectively portrays just how slippery that slope can really be, how easy it is for a person to go from privilege to poverty, from life to death, sometimes so gradually that you never even see it coming. The characterization is deep, often affectionate, always allowing you judge for yourself. The writing is stark, honest, and stripped-down, making no excuses, just like the classic punk [music] that sees frequent mention throughout.

—*Broken Pencil Magazine*

With a bright beamed flashlight, Danila Botha investigates the cracks in her characters' messy and poignant lives. Her stories are disturbing, honest and sad. She has a real talent for expressing raw emotion and vulnerability.

—Michelle McGrane

Things That Cause Inappropriate Happiness

Short Stories

ESSENTIAL PROSE SERIES 216

Canada

Guernica Editions Inc. acknowledges the support of
the Canada Council for the Arts and the Ontario Arts Council.
The Ontario Arts Council is an agency of the Government of Ontario.

We acknowledge the financial support of the Government of Canada.

DANILA BOTHA

Things That Cause Inappropriate Happiness

Short Stories

GUERNICA EDITIONS

TORONTO • CHICAGO
BUFFALO • LANCASTER (U.K.)
2024

Guernica Founder: Antonio D'Alfonso

Michael Mirolla, editor

Interior and cover design: Rafael Chimicatti
Cover image: karina tess/unsplash
Guernica Editions Inc.
287 Templemead Drive, Hamilton, ON L8W 2W4
2250 Military Road, Tonawanda, N.Y. 14150-6000 U.S.A.
www.guernicaeditions.com

Distributors:
Independent Publishers Group (IPG)
600 North Pulaski Road, Chicago IL 60624
University of Toronto Press Distribution (UTP)
5201 Dufferin Street, Toronto (ON), Canada M3H 5T8

First edition.
Printed in Canada.

Legal Deposit—First Quarter
Library of Congress Catalog Card Number: 2023944361
Library and Archives Canada Cataloguing in Publication
Title: Things that cause inappropriate happiness : short stories /
Danila Botha.
Names: Botha, Danila, 1982- author.
Series: Essential prose series ; 216.
Description: Series statement: Essential prose series ; 216
Identifiers: Canadiana (print) 20230522858 | Canadiana (ebook)
20230522882 | ISBN 9781771838702 (softcover)
ISBN 9781771838719 (EPUB)
Classification: LCC PS8603.O915 T55 2024 | DDC C813/.6—dc23

Contents

Sometimes I Like to Shoot Kids

YESTERDAY MORNING I got to school forty-five minutes early only to find four kids having a fist fight. All I could see was tiny fists flying, and two boys lying on their backs outside my classroom. It was easier to identify them first: Liron and Maor. Liron was wearing his bright green T-shirt and Maor was yelling. It took me a minute to realize what was happening.

Yasmin and Jana, two tiny, beautiful girls, were sitting on their chests, punching them. Jana even got a right hook to Maor's cheek. There was a part of me that hesitated to break it up. Liron and Maor were the kinds of pains in the ass that mercilessly mocked other students. The school was located on the second floor above a Pizza Hut, a grocery store and a McDonald's, and Liron spent his first recess whipping glass bottles at passing cars.

"What the hell do you think you're doing?" I asked him, trying my best to be some kind of authority figure.

He shrugged and looked at me. "Aiming for the windshield, Tamar."

I took a deep breath and got the principal. "I'm not cut out for this," I told her.

She shrugged. "You'll be fine. You've just been in America for too long. You'll get used to it."

Canada, I thought, but didn't correct her. I've been living in Canada.

"Girls," I said carefully. "Get off them."

The boys jumped up and ran away. "Not that I'm sure that they didn't deserve it," I said while they were still in earshot.

I looked at Yasmin and Jana. "What happened?"

Jana looked at me with her big brown eyes. Her long dark ponytail had almost come out of its elastic.

"The usual stuff, Tamar. They want to bomb our village. Shoot us. You know."

I looked at her. They were the only Arab-Israeli kids in the class. They were cousins.

Yasmin grew up in Jerusalem, and Jana lived in Jaljulye. They went to regular Israeli public schools. In the breaks from class they spoke Hebrew to each other.

"I just, I couldn't take it anymore. Someone had to tell them. It was enough already."

I hugged her. "Of course," I said. "I understand, believe me. But I don't want you to get into trouble with the school. Just tell me if they say anything like that again. I'll take care of it."

Yasmin join us in our hug.

I knew what would happen when I spoke to the boys. They'd laugh and their parents would be defensive and dismissive. The principal would do nothing unless someone seriously got hurt. I took a deep breath and walked into my classroom. I controlled the urge to punch a hole through my paper-thin walls.

I taught English as a Second Language beside the bookstore, across from a record store.

For the past few months, I'd been teaching adults but the in the summer they run an English summer camp for kids of all ages. I figured it would be less depressing than teaching people who were only a year or two older than me who were studying English to travel or do their Masters degrees in North America or England.

I had no plans. I'd been studying art and photography in Jerusalem but I decided to take a break. It was a competitive program and I wasn't sure what I was going to do afterwards.

My mom thought I should finish my degree and become an art teacher or come back to Canada and do a different degree. I moved in with my cousins, in the town I grew up in, and got a job at a nearby school. It seemed like a good way to see if I wanted to teach.

Every day I doubted it more.

Some days I kind of liked my job.

The kindergarten kids were my favourite. There were Michal and Yoni, whose mothers were best friends, who told me everyday that they wanted to marry each other when they grew up. Sometimes they even held hands under the table. There was Mohammed, the gentle, well mannered little boy whose mother frets that he is being disrespectful. There was Maya, a little genius who could already read in Hebrew and was eager to learn to read in English. It was rare anywhere, to find a kid who really wanted to learn for the sake of learning. There were also Shira's mom, who reminded me every morning to give Shira her Ritalin in the class break.

Sometimes it was a lot to remember.

I watched reality TV and took photos in my free time.

Sometimes I tortured myself by going into the bookstore and flirting with the guy who worked behind the cash. His name was Bar. He didn't talk much, and when he did it tended to be sarcastic. We flirted for a few weeks, and when I finally thought—I can't do this anymore, if he doesn't ask me out soon, I'm going to ask him—he casually mentioned that he had a girlfriend. Now when he sees me, he looks both happy and guilty so it's less masochistic than it sounds.

I don't even know what I like about him, apart from the fact that he puts aside photography books for me, and he's read just about every book ever written.

I've become friends with the guy who works in the record store. His name is Yaron and he has blue eyes and long thick eyelashes. He has sandy hair that springs into tightly wound curls. I guess I'm not his type, although I have no idea what his type is.

Some kind of hippie? Someone with flowing skirts and glasses? Someone who reads philosophy instead of photography books and short stories.

Sometimes when he smiles at me I think he thinks of me as a little sister.

I guess I should be happy that he's not predatory.

We've started taking our lunch breaks at the same time now. He asked me about Canada and I asked him about travelling in Asia.

"What's Laos like?" I asked one day.

"Like Israel on Yom Kippur, but like, every day."

I raised an eyebrow. "You mean the country just comes to a standstill?"

He smiled. "It's very quiet."

One day he came with me to the pet store across the street to play with the puppies. The guy in the store asked me if he was my boyfriend and I shook my head. He looked confused but I just shrugged.

Today Bar showed up at my work and asked me to go for lunch. We walked through the restaurants below, the Burger Ranch and McDonald's and sweaty Schnitzels that had been sitting on plates for hours.

There were a couple of food stands outside.

"Let's get *sambusek*," he said, and I nodded.

I bit into the hot dough and ran my tongue along my teeth to pick out sesame seeds. It was forty degrees out.

"What happened to your girlfriend?" I asked.

"We broke up like a week ago," he said. "Don't worry about it."

He tried to kiss me at the bottom of the stairs going up to the school. I pulled back. I had no intention of making it that easy.

"You can text me later," I said. "I'm done teaching at 4pm." I laughed all the way into my classroom.

By the end of the day, he'd texted me five times.

I felt guilty so I called him.

"Want to see a movie tomorrow night?" he asked.

"Sure."

"I have some good movies at my house. Maybe you should come over."

"Okay," I said.

I spent the next morning taking photos of the kids splashing in puddles across the street from the apartment. There was an elementary school whose bells rang to the tune of "Santa Claus is Coming to Town."

Yaron came to visit me that afternoon on my break. He sat down in the staff room, and he flipped through the book of photography Bar had given me recently. It was called *Drive By Shootings*, a series of black and white photos taken by a New York taxi driver.

I smiled. A kid's class was going on outside, and a couple of them were screaming.

"It would be so cool to have my own book like this someday."

He looked at me. "You will." He paused. "What'll it be about?"

I grinned. "Kids, obviously."

"You need a good title."

Outside, another kid screamed.

"I'll get back to you," I said and he smiled.

"Okay. I'm waiting to hear."

I walked back with him to the record store. He made funny mistakes with English speaking customers. "Thank you so much," one of them said. "You're mostly welcome," he answered, and I tried not to laugh.

After work he drove me but he didn't want to come upstairs. My cousins were starting to think there was something going on so I told them about my date with Bar.

He came to pick me up an hour later.

He lived with his parents in an apartment a few streets away.

He kissed me. He had full lips. Come on," he said, and led me to his bedroom.

The blinds were closed and it was full of shelf after shelf of books. A part of me wanted to go through them more than wanted to talk to him.

He flopped down on the faded blue comforter on his bed and pulled me on top of him.

After months of waiting it was weird for things to move so fast.

He pulled my shirt up over my head. "I wanted you since the day you walked into the store," he said. I laughed. "What? I did."

"It took you long enough," I answered and he laughed.

He was pulling my pants off when his mom walked into the room.

She saw my white underwear and red lace bra before I'd even been introduced.

"Hi," she said, as I scrambled to throw his blanket over myself.

She looked away until I got dressed.

"Bar's mentioned you," she said in English. "Would you like to stay for dinner?"

My parents are Canadians who waged an English speaking war in our home, especially at meal times. My brother and I would speak to each other in Hebrew at the table, and our parents would demand we answer them in English or wouldn't get dessert.

Bar's mother is American. His parents separated for a few years after his dad got his secretary pregnant, but they'd been back together for five years. His brother was married and had a five-year-old daughter. On Friday nights they did family dinners, less out of a religious obligation and more out of convenience.

I nodded slowly. "Okay."

His mom made crispy chicken, roast potatoes and salad.

I spent most of the meal playing with his niece, Amit. Her parents had been trying to have another child for four years, and the tension between them was obvious. I tried not to think about Bar telling me, matter-of-factly, that his brother saw a prostitute on Allenby in Tel Aviv every two weeks, to "release tension." Bar himself had lost his virginity to a Russian prostitute named Irina when he was in the army. "It was embarrassing to still be a virgin at nineteen," he said. He stopped going after a few months, when he realized he'd fallen in love with her.

I took out my camera and took a few photos of Amit. She giggled and started posing. I talked to her, to distract her, so instead of making duck faces, I could capture her personality.

I tried to avoid making eye contact with his mother.

Bar reached for my hand under the table.

"So Tamar," his dad, said eventually, "what is it that you do?"

I looked at him. "I work at Wall Street Institute."

His dad seemed impressed and looked at Bar.

"She's in finance?"

Bar snorted. "It's the name of a language school. She teaches English, but she's an artist."

I shrugged. "I guess so. I like to take photos."

They looked at me expectantly.

"Sometimes I think about putting together a collection of photos for an art show. There's a gallery in South Tel Aviv that's been interested after I sent them some work. I'm trying to put together some of my latest stuff for them."

Bar looked at me. "What's it about?"

"The show?"

He nodded and they all turned towards me.

I looked at his parents. I thought of all the kids and their parents. I thought Liron and Maor, of Yasmin and Jana

"Kids," I said quietly. "I find them fascinating."

His mother smiled at me.

"There's something about them that's so open, whether they're ecstatic or angry or upset, if they're being mean or sweet or annoying, their reactions are always so authentic." I looked away. "I'm thinking of calling it sometimes I like to shoot kids." I cracked a small smile.

Everybody was silent.

I heard the clink of the knife as it scraped against Bar's mother's plate. His father stared at me.

Eventually, Bar let out a low and gravelly laugh.

I pulled my hand away from his and got up.

I walked into the hallway and texted Yaron.

Soulmates

HER NAME WAS RICKIE. She was named after an Aunt Rivka in her dad's family but she found the name, which just meant Rebecca in Yiddish, too straight out of the *shtetl*, so she went by Rickie. "Like Rickie Lee Jones," her mom would sometimes tell people, and we'd smile politely because it seemed like the right thing to do.

One time her mom serenaded us with *Chuck E's In Love*, which didn't really help. I asked my parents, and they didn't know who Rickie Lee Jones was either, but I was used to that. When you're raised Orthodox Jewish, like my mom was, and you go to an all-girl's school that you later teach at, and you get married at twenty and start having kids, you don't have much chance to be different. I was the oldest of five. My dad, like Rickie's mom, was a *Baal Teshuva*, meaning someone who wasn't raised with religion but returned to God. He had great stories that he'd tell my sisters and I before bed, and even better stories that he'd tell me when we went for walks. Our lives were so regimented, with school, family and social obligations that his stories felt like fairy tales, too good to be real.

My sisters' favourite story was the one about the horse. My dad loved horses, and he and his brother took a bus out to the country, with all their money saved to answer an ad they'd read. Some guy was willing to sell them an old, dusty white horse, but the saddle cost almost as much and they could afford one or the other. They chose the horse, figuring they could build a saddle out of the awful leather jacket their parents had given my dad for his birthday. When they got home, their mom threatened to send the horse to the glue factory, so they sold it to a neighbour.

When we went for walks alone, my dad would tell me things about my mom that I never knew: how she'd always wanted to try lobster, how the smell of it cooking in butter made her momentarily rethink keeping kosher for the first time in her life, and when she was nineteen, she wanted to get a yellow butterfly tattooed on her right ankle. I knew the fact that my dad was newly religious appealed to my mom.

"His love of Judaism is so pure," I heard her tell my aunt one day. "When we first met, it was like watching a kid discover the kind of small miracles you take for granted."

Once he told me about a miscarriage my mom had months before she got pregnant with me. "You're our miracle baby, that's why we called you Nessa," he said. "Nessa" means "miracle of God" in Hebrew. "Then after you, *Baruch Hashem*, everything was easy."

It was a big decision on their part to send me and my sister to a co-ed Jewish high school. He wanted us to go to university and have actual careers.

One of my dad's friends told him that no respectable guy from our community would ever want to marry us if we went there.

I secretly hoped that his friend was right.

When I became friends with Rickie, my parents assumed she was religious because of her name. She was always dressed appropriately in front of them, which made me laugh. After she turned twelve, her parents gave her a choice, so she wore jeans and tank tops, went out on Shabbat and only ate kosher in front of them. Her crew of non-Jewish friends from her neighbourhood called her Becky. I never corrected them.

She had a birthday dance party in the basement of a kosher restaurant, but all I told my parents was a kosher restaurant so they let me go.

There was a dinner set up upstairs. Rickie walked in, wearing a short satin-y yellow dress, and her black hair pulled back with a red hair band. I always thought she looked a little like snow white, but tonight, with her skin looking extra pale, and her lips shellacked red to match her hairband, she really did.

I looked down. A few days before, I told Rickie I had nothing to wear. Rickie brought me a whole wardrobe of clothes like the best friend in a sitcom to try on. In the end, I wore my own white T-shirt, her jeans and a jacket that I kept all the way zipped up.

I shellacked my cheeks with green Jerome Russell body glitter and the first thing she said when she saw me was that I was the shiniest person she'd ever seen.

"Is that good?" I asked her.

"Of course. When I think of you, I always think, sparkling, and now other people can see it too."

Rickie sat beside me, and ordered a million things, matzoh ball soup, grilled chicken on a bun, fries, pastrami sandwich, and took a few small bites of each, then said she was full.

I ordered chicken fingers, like I always did when I ate there.

I used to always get wings in a basket with fries, but one time when I was younger I ordered it and accidentally swallowed part of the small bone.

We were with our next-door neighbours, and I'd done this thing of breaking off a small piece from the middle of a loaf of breadbasket bread. The mom embarrassed me in a way that confused me at first, pretending she was empathizing by saying 'I know it's kind of a fun thing to do' when really she was calling me out. She leaned in when I started choking. Maybe she thought I was faking it. She told me to settle down, but I couldn't breathe, and I couldn't talk. My parents rushed me to the ER, and we never socialized with them again.

I tried to eat as daintily as Rickie had, but I kept dropping my chicken fingers, and she kept laughing at me.

Later that night, we hung out with her other friends, at a park near her house and I got drunk for the first time. After the others left, we sat side by side on the bridge of a big jungle gym.

She'd lost her hairband and eyeliner was pooled under her eyes.

"You're so beautiful," I said, and she kissed me. Her lips were soft and felt electric. For a few minutes, it felt like there was glitter in my bloodstream. It's rare when something you've imagined for ages turns out better in real life. I wanted to take a thousand photos of her, of us, of the playground, anything so I could keep replaying how it all felt. This is what a real miracle feels like, I thought.

I started to talk, to try to tell her that but she leaned forward and threw up all over the big plastic red slide. I leaned in and tried to hold her hair back.

After that, I walked her home but nothing else happened. When we got to her door, she thanked me for being such a good friend.

I thought about it as I walked back to my neighbourhood. I thought about my parents and figured it was probably just as well. I had no idea what they would do if they found out. Moving me to a more religious school where I'd be surrounded by all girls didn't exactly seem like a punishment. I knew they wouldn't know how to deal with it. They lived in a world where gender roles were so prescribed. Even their personal tastes were like that. My mom loved lace and romance novels. My dad didn't think women should drink beer. My mom wouldn't let me drive until I was eighteen. I knew I wouldn't be able to fake it forever. I knew one day I wouldn't be the daughter that they wanted.

We didn't avoid each other after that, but we didn't talk about it either. She'd hug me, and for a few minutes after, my clothes would smell like the vanilla amber perfume oil she rolled on her neck and in her hair. It was important to her that we still acted like friends. I didn't want to be a creep that hung all over her, all love struck and desperate, so I kept my distance.

I focused on school. I babysat my siblings. I let my mom sign me up as one of the babysitters at our synagogue's Shabbat daycare. I even went on a few awkward dates that my mom's matchmaker friend set me up with. My lack of interest made me seem pious and modest, so naturally they all wanted second dates, but I refused.

My mom wanted me to go to seminary in Israel for a year, and I agreed, knowing that I planned to drop out after a few weeks and move in with my not religious at all cousins, who had already agreed to it.

My cousins lived in Tel Aviv, and they figured me out right away, even when I was too afraid to say it.

They took me out to gay bars and dance clubs. I went to my first Pride Parade.

I went out on real dates. I had sex for the first time. After almost a year, I finally had a girlfriend. Her name was Linnea, and she was Swedish, and not Jewish. She was doing her master's at Tel Aviv university in public health. She had a different perspective on everything. Together we volunteered with both Israeli and Palestinian kids. I started thinking in depth about both sides of the history here for the first time.

A few months later, I got a message from Rickie. She was living in Jerusalem now, going to a seminary.

She wanted to meet up, and I was shocked when I saw her. She was wearing a floor length denim skirt and a loose, striped long sleeved blue and white shirt, even though it was ninety degrees out. Her dark hair was shorter and pulled back in a messy ponytail.

"You look so different," she kept saying. "You look taller."

I was dressed casually, shorts and a green tank top, so my tattoos were all visible. I had a small rainbow tattoo on my right inner wrist. I got the butterfly on my ankle that I knew my mom would never get. I hadn't spoken to my family in months. I had a line from a Fiona Apple song across my left shoulder, in beautiful, looping script.

"*Be kind to me/or treat me mean/I'll make the most of it/I'm an extraordinary machine.*"

She didn't ask me anything but I found myself blurting it out, desperate to see her reaction.

I told her all about Linnea. "She's so smart, and interesting. I never thought I'd meet someone who would love me too."

She looked sad. "Everyone has a Jewish soulmate," she said, and it sounded absurd, like that 80's animated movie, *All Dogs Go to Heaven*.

"So if my girlfriend was Jewish, you'd be okay with me being gay?"

She shook her head, started to talk, then stopped herself.

"I'm getting married," she said, and looked me in the eye for the first time.

"Wow. *Mazel tov*," I sputtered.

"Who's the lucky guy?"

"His name is Chezi. Short for Yechezkel."

"Wow."

"How well do you know this guy?"

"Pretty well. We've gone on three dates. I know all the stuff that matters. I met him after I went on a date with his friend."

Her eyes light up for the first time. "He was this guy from Brazil, so cute and so interesting. We went out twice, and the first time he told the matchmaker how much he liked me. I have no idea what happened."

I wanted to tell her that everyone gets rejected, that it was ridiculous to marry someone's friend just because the person you wanted jilted you. Instead, I reached over and hugged her.

I expected her to flinch, but she didn't. She pulled me closer and told me I smelled fresh, like the ocean.

We stood there for what felt like hours, hugging each other. She kissed me on the forehead, and it still felt a tiny bit magical, like a stray piece of glitter that I couldn't wash off no matter how many times I tried.

Don't Look Back

My great aunt Mara was the one who taught me what nominative determinism was. My grandfather made the joke once, when he heard me asking my grandmother what she was like as a kid. What can you expect, he asked, and smiled his slightly crooked half-smile.

Mara, I knew, meant bitter.

Great aunt Mara's real name was Tamara, but no one ever called her that. Tamara came from the word Tamar, which meant date, like the fruit. I sometimes wondered after that, what would have happened if her parents and older siblings had been more patient, if she would have been as soft, and yielding and honey toned as a medjool date if they'd stuck to calling her that.

My mom always hated the way she gleefully interrupted people to correct their grammar. If I ever told her she was using a word wrong, she'd say, "That's enough," and then add: "You don't want to be like Auntie Mara." For my mom Mara was always a cautionary tale. I thought she was misunderstood, but even her own kids and their father kept their distance.

I tried to picture Mara as a kid, but all I could see was her today, small, with slightly curved shoulders, determined to make the tiny bronze busts on her work desk conform fully to her vision. Her face looked exactly like a portrait I'd seen of my great grandmother, but I could never tell if I really remembered her or if it was everyone else's stories and the framed photos my whole family had of her in their houses.

Mara was the only real artist I knew. When I applied and got into art school, and my mom mentioned it to her, she seemed excited, which was something, since no one else thought it was so great. I went to the kind of high school that forced me to figure things out early. It was mostly a sad thing, when I thought about how much of my teenage years I spent agonizing about things I couldn't possibly know, but in some ways it made things simpler. My scores on our standardized tests were high enough. I could have got into other programs, the kind my parents desperately wished I chose instead, but when I thought about them, the only image that made me happy was me sitting in a studio with headphones on, painting all day.

Mara made me promise that I'd take a few philosophy courses if I could, and a few literature courses. She was the only one of her siblings who had a master's degree, and the only one who couldn't make a decent living. She took odd jobs, and sometimes she even had normal ones, like teaching little kids at a daycare, or teaching art in an art college, but it was never enough, and my grandparents often supported her. I asked her once if it bothered her, and she shrugged. "We all contribute in different ways," she said. "My art will be here after me." When she could sell her work, her bronze sculptures, her ceramics, her portraits, she always sold them for a lot of money, but it didn't happen often enough.

She was proud of me, I knew, for getting accepted into an art school in the US. She'd spent time in other places, in

South Africa, in Australia, even in Canada, but she always came back to our small town in Israel.

"Make it work," she whispered to me before I went. "Make a life for yourself. There's much more opportunity there. Don't look back."

I wanted to be like her, unshakeably confident in who I was, and what I was creating. But I wasn't.

I came back both summers, after my first and second year. I missed my parents and my sisters. Once a week on Wednesdays in the summers, our town had an outdoor market called a Yarid, where everyone from little kids making bead necklaces to silversmiths making fancy rings with turquoise and coral sold their wares. Naturally, Aunt Mara was there, selling her ceramic bowls and nude bronze ladies in various states of repose. I still went to my favourite art store, the only one in our town, on our main street where everything was overpriced, and they didn't have the high series cobalt blues or lime greens I'd come to love, but Pazit, the poufy haired, eternally bored owner, greeted me with the same friendly indifference as before, never asking me about my time in America, and I could pretend for a few minutes that nothing had changed. But when I got home and sat on my family's balcony, in my usual chair, headphones blasting music so loudly you could hear it if you stood close to me, I knew I'd lost the freedom I used to have, when no one expected me to do anything except quietly amuse myself. I had my professor's voices in my head with every brushstroke, I could hear the group critiques and suddenly the stakes were high. I had to make a success of my life there; I had to justify the money that was being spent on me; I had to make everything work somehow.

I ended up tearing page after page out of my sketchbook, and I destroyed two canvases midway through. I used to hate our building's giant garbage shoot when I was younger, but I loved it now. I could fit canvases into black garbage bags and make them disappear without having to explain myself. Aunt Mara insisted I come with her on Wednesday nights to help her sell. On the nights that we didn't sell anything, I was disappointed. I'd ask Mara if she didn't think her work was overpriced. I was sure that if we lowered the prices by a third, even by half that we'd sell it all.

She glared at me, her black olive eyes glinting with startling sparks.

She pointed an arthritic finger at my face. "You always have to know your worth, child. If you don't, who will? I'd rather sell nothing than to devalue my work."

I stared at her, trying to decide if I admired her or thought she was crazy. After that, she made me come with her to start selling my own work. I didn't have much with me, except whatever was in my portfolio that I'd brought from New York. I had to admit, people's compliments felt good, even if they didn't buy anything. My expectations were low, and if someone bought something even with Aunt Mara inflating its worth, it felt incredible.

When I was packing to go back to school, Aunt Mara tapped me on the shoulder.

"I helped you a lot this summer, didn't I?" she asked, with an arch smile I'd not seen before.

I nodded.

She then gave me a big black zip up bag full of her art, including small bronze and carefully bubble wrapped ceramic sculptures, and a detailed price list.

"See if you can get some Americans to bite," she said.

The thought of lugging the bag back with me seemed like a nightmare, but I couldn't afford to throw the stuff away and pay for it myself. I told one of my professors that I had some art from a famous Israeli artist, and she agreed to feature it in an upcoming student and alumna show.

Aunt Mara was losing her hearing, just like everyone else in my mom's family, but when I told her about it over What's App, and she finally understood me, she was ecstatic.

She insisted on flying there for the opening, which seemed a bit over the top for a show that served blocks of no name cheese and crackers, but she was so happy. My professor set it up to center on a piece that was not typical of her style and I tried to explain that, but he ignored me. It was a bust, of a mother and child. The child's eyes were squeezed shut, the rest of its expression a grimace. The mother looks down, tears coming out of her eyes. It was uncharacteristically vulnerable. The rest of her work was all about female sexuality, female confidence, "what your generation would call feminist and sex positive," she'd say and flinch a little. I'd never seen anything like the mother and child, and I wondered why she'd included it. But my teachers loved it, so I gave in and deferred to their expertise.

It was my parents who paid for her plane ticket. Aunt Mara stayed in my apartment with me, for a few days, running a broom over the floors absently, making tea and then forgetting to drink it.

The night of the show, she was nervous. She changed three times into various versions of the loose floral dresses she loved and changed her shoes twice. She wore a ceramic beaded necklace with one of her tiny sculptures as the centre piece. She even asked me to help her put on make up, some rose blush on cheeks, gold eye shadow to highlight her intense eyes.

When we got there, she moved around the room, seeming taller and more beautiful than ever. She let someone pour her a glass of white wine and got annoyed when I asked her if alcohol interacted with any of her medications. Someone bought one of her full-figured ceramic women and she was delighted and then a pregnant woman, with a toddler hanging onto her skirt, edged her way towards the mother and child. It was the only piece without an artist statement beside it. She looked at my aunt Mara, her eyes filling with tears.

"It's such a perfect metaphor for parenting," she said. "No matter what we do, everything is a risk but we keep trying and we keep loving. I promised my husband I wasn't going to buy anything, but what the hell."

Aunt Mara exhaled so sharply everyone heard it. People standing close to us turned around to listen.

"My dear," she said, her voice growing louder with each syllable. "That is not what my piece is about at all. The reason I chose not to write an artist statement was exactly that; fear of being reduced to the banal."

It seemed like everyone was listening now. I looked down at my sneakers.

"When I was your age," she said, then looked the woman up and down. "No, when I was younger than you, I had two healthy children and I was already pregnant with my third. My second child, my son, Moshe, got meningitis, and there were no vaccines and the doctors couldn't do anything and he died."

I looked up at her. No one had ever told me this story. My family had obliquely referred to hard times she'd had when she was younger, but her kids all had issues, and different fathers, so I assumed I knew everything, more or less.

Aunt Mara stared at the woman, who seemed to shrink before our eyes.

"It's not about parenthood, my dear. It's about losing the most precious things we have, and being powerless to stop it."

The woman backed away, and walked out the door, her son whining behind her.

People went back to their conversations, everyone trying to pretend that nothing had ever happened here, that the night could still be a success. She didn't sell anything else.

A few days later, she packed up all her stuff, and got ready to head home.

As we waited for her cab, she took my hand, and thanked me for the trip.

"Why did you never tell me?" I asked her quietly.

She sighed. "I talked about it at the time. After a while, people stopped wanting to hear about it, and I stopped wanting to hear their platitudes."

"Is that what you afraid of?" I asked, practically whispering. "Did you think I was just like everyone else?"

She pulled me close to her and put her hands on both sides of my face.

"You, my darling, are the most unique, talented artist of us all. You're going to do great things. I was trying to find the right time to tell you. It shouldn't have been that night."

It was the closest I'd ever heard her come to an apology. I found myself crying.

I hoped she wasn't disappointed when I found that I had nothing to say, no comfort, no insights.

I helped load her suitcase into the trunk of her cab, and she rolled down the window and waved to me.

"Never waste any time feeling guilty."

When the car pulled away, I thought I heard her add, "I love you," but I might have imagined it.

My mom and dad were the I love you types, and Aunt Mara was the succinct type, but I knew I felt it.

Dark and Lilac Fairies

When I turned twelve, my parents who weren't all that religious decided I needed to have an over the top, lavish bat mitzvah. All the other Jewish girls were having functions and banquets, practically every other weekend, but I wanted nothing to do with it. It was my *Nagymama*, who as a little kid I just called *Mama*, who convinced me. She lived with us, and raised me while my parents worked, so if there was one opinion I listened to, it was hers.

"In this life," she said, in her soft Hungarian accent, "you never know what could happen. If you have an opportunity to celebrate, you must take it."

We decided to make the theme around ballet. We convinced my parents to rent the performance space from the dance studio I practised in. Instead of a fancy sit down dinner, there would be hors d'oeuvres and music, culminating in a dance performance where I would be the star.

It took a lot of arm twisting, but I convinced her to participate too.

Before the war, *Nagymama* was in training to be a ballerina. Her older sister, Perla Markovics had danced with the Hungarian National Ballet. There were photos of her in frames on *Nagymama*'s bedside table, looking impossibly elegant and self possessed, the kind of person everyone wants to be. She died heroically in the war, but it was the discipline and training she taught her, *Nagymama* insisted, that kept her alive.

She still had the slight build and gently sculpted muscles of a ballerina. She always sat perfectly straight, like she had a rod propping up her spine. When we had a barre installed in our basement, so I could practice, she practiced with me. When she came to pick me up from dance school, she wore eyeliner, mascara and blush. My teacher Oksana loved her the most. "She's so elegant," she said to me one day while she finished her cigarette before class. "Classic European beauty."

My mom, by contrast, was *zaftig* to use *Nagymama*'s word. She had stubby fingers that were always greasy with eucalyptus hand cream, because she insisted they were dry, even in the summer. *Nagymama* said they looked sausages about to burst in a frying pan.

We decided to do *Sleeping Beauty*, because it was my favourite. I always found it hard to get out of bed in the mornings, and I often woke up with *Nagymama* siting beside me, stroking my hair, saying "*Jó reggelt*, Sleeping Beauty." Or if she was feeling extra affectionate, "*Gut Morgen, Shayna Maidel.*"

Nagymama didn't speak Yiddish very often. She was the only person in her family left after the war, and she trained and landed a place in the National Ballet. She lived on her own in Budapest for a few years before she met my grandfather and came to Canada. She didn't want me to call her *Bubbe* because she was superstitious.

Between Oxana and I, we convinced her to play the Lilac Fairy.

They projected baby photos of me, and my lawyer parents, gamely dressed as the king and queen stood beside the huge screen.

My friends from dance school played all the different Fairies: Tenderness, Playfulness, Generosity, Serenity, and Courage. Five beautiful twirling fairies, in Jordan almond pastel colours, baby pink, light blue, mint green, light yellow, and dark pink.

Days before the party, Sandra, who was supposed to play the Fairy of Darkness, got Mono.

After a lot of convincing, *Nagymama* agreed to play both parts.

"You know, it sort of makes sense," I said to her, the night before the party. "That you could be both fairies, darkness and light."

Splotches of red appeared on her cheeks. "You think I like the darkness?"

I thought about stories she'd told me about the games she'd played with other Jewish kids during the war. "*Jews and Gestapo*," she'd said. "Two of us were Gestapo, the rest were Jews. We had to catch them and arrest them. Tie them up and hit them."

"Who were you?" I'd asked her, and she'd flinched.

"The Gestapo. I was always the Gestapo."

Another one was called *Klepsi-Klepsi*. One kid was blindfolded, "with whatever *shmatte* we could find" and the other kids took turns hitting them in the face as hard as they could. When the blindfold came off, the kid had to guess who'd hit them.

Nagymama had the best poker face. She shrugged when I looked horrified.

"If someone has to hit you, better it should be your friend."

I thought about the storage room downstairs, all the extra food and clothes, she kept, "just to make sure."

My dad would tell her to stop hoarding, and she'd fix him with her most withering stare and mutter: "*Es art mikh vi di kats fun mitvokh.*" I care like a cat cares that it's Wednesday.

"I don't think you like the darkness," I said carefully. "I think you like to be prepared for anything."

She smiled. "I think you're right," she said.

As the Dark Fairy, she moved with heavy limbs, her black and gold robes shaking.

She cursed me to prick my finger on a spindle and die, cringing as she spoke.

As the Lilac Fairy, in her lavender dress and shoes, she moved with ease, lessening the curse, saying she wished she could take it on herself, take it away all together.

Her hair was twisted up with tortoise shell clips her mother had bought in Paris in the old days. They'd sat in her drawer, along with a yellowing article about her sister, for as long as I could remember.

The rest of the dance moved quickly. I did all the moves I'd worked so hard on, including the jetes, and two minutes of the Rose Adagio. People clapped.

A handsome male ballerina was the prince who kissed me and woke me up.

Everyone talked about what a unique and amazing experience it was.

For my gift, *Nagymama* gave me a pair of rose gold stud earrings.

I waited until I was in bed that night to read her card:

Penny, Mayne Hartzeleh,

You are my *Oytser*, my greatest treasure. These earrings used to belong to Perla. One of her ballerina friends gave them back to me after the war.

I know you know the story, of how Perla danced to entertain the soldiers at Auschwitz. How they gave her extra food, cigarettes, and squares of chocolate that kept me alive. You know the famous part of the story, how when she was selected, she flirted with the Nazi guard, got his gun and shot him. You know that she injured some other Nazi too, and all the women started fighting back, but they were all gassed in the end. I was changed forever that day, and not just because she was a hero. That day, it finally registered that the thick smoke that turned the sky red was more than just chemicals. I understood I was never going to see my mama, or sisters or father again. The smell of skin melting is like the smell of burning feathers. I wanted to grip her hand and never let go. But I lived. I danced. And I helped to raise you.

I know you have her talent and her bravery. I hope you also have my will to survive, to be prepared for anything, no matter what happens.

I wiped away the tears with the back of my hand and hid the card in the corner of my bookshelf where I knew my parents would never look. They really wanted us to be normal, to pretend that the world was safe, that if we were good, and happy, we had control over what happened to us.

We all have both Dark and Lilac Fairies in us, I wanted to tell them, but I knew they wouldn't understand. *Nagymama* would. I tried to remember all my thoughts so I could tell her in the morning.

Able to Pass

IT DIDN'T TAKE MUCH to remember what she'd heard, because of all the Jewish traditions this was the strangest. Judaism insisted that you couldn't mix wool and linen, that owning pigeons made you an ineligible witness, and that waving a live chicken around your head before Rosh Hashana was the best way to get rid of that year's sins, and yet here she was. She almost started to laugh, but she'd caught her grandmother's eye. Her *Bubbe*, who floated in and out of the Toronto winter, and the Polish countryside. They would sit on her green velvet couch, swallowed by pillows, her grandmother's PSW Anita waiting to bring them tea with lemon and sugar, and rugelach bursting with poppy seeds. Her *Bubbe*, with her intense eyes, which could change from a winter blue to the softer, muddier melt of a spring river. She didn't say I love you much, but Kayla understood when she was being nagged to eat more lokshen kugel or dry, crumbly honey cake, to wear a scarf even when she wasn't cold but especially when her *Bubbe* wanted to tell her things she'd never told anyone else.

"We tried to build a golem," she'd said the last time Kayla visited.

"A what?"

"A golem. Me and Golda. We didn't know the right words, but Golda had a friend, a secret boyfriend who'd been learning at the yeshiva, so she knew some. We made her from dust and the mud at the riverbank."

She looked Kayla in the eye and waved her hand. "A creature. You know, a creature that looks like a person. You make them from clay, or mud, and then in time ..."

"What?"

"They begin to exist."

Her *Bubbe* laughed, and the collection of colourful and kitschy Matryoshka dolls on the windowsill behind her caught Kayla's eye. Inside one of them were small odds and ends that survived the war with her: her mother's ring, a bead from her sister's necklace, tiny notes that could fit under her tongue.

"They're not quite the same as us, you know, but they look human. And they protect us. That's their job."

"What exactly were you planning to do?" Kayla blurted out before she could stop herself.

"Oh, I don't know, darling," she answered. "People were disappearing everyday. There was a rumour, you know, a young man who escaped and came back, all hanging skin and bones and missing nails, he hid with the dead bodies on the train, then with the luggage that was being sent back—he said he heard that they were looking for twins. Our father was gone by then, so we couldn't decide if it we'd be saved or hunted if we stayed. We thought we could replace ourselves so our real versions could hide."

She shook her head, a faint half smile playing on her lips, and Kayla tried not to stare. If it had worked, she realized, *Bubbe's* sister would have survived and their family wouldn't have been so tiny.

That night, Kayla started to research. She'd learned about it in school, of course, and she had her grandmother's fragments, but she started to read about her grandmother's village in Southern Poland. She read about *Sefer Hayitzirah,* and other sources of Jewish magic and mysticism. She read *The Clay Boy* and *The Puttermesser Papers*. She even reread *Frankenstein*.

She had photos of her grandmother from before the war, back when she was Basja Dawidowicz, Basza to her Polish friends, blonde and blue eyed, tall and social, able to pass. Her mother Lejka died when she was ten, and Basja was jealous sometimes, that her mother got to miss the suffering, and that their town, and family and friends were frozen in a state of comfort and mendacity in her mind. Basja could have hidden, but all she had left was her delicate, dark-haired twin. Her brilliant sister, the punch line of many family jokes. "I should have been named Golda," she could hear her *Bubbe* say, "look at my hair, my personality, when the real Golda was always so serious ..."

Kayla was an art major who minored in accounting to keep her parents happy. Her *Bubbe* had told her once that her name meant vessel of God, that being able to create things was her gift.

She drew the family members first, with pencil and charcoal, slowly adding colour.

She ordered bags of clay, spray bottles for water, elephant ear sponges, potter ribs and toggle clay cutters. She would make them all fit inside each other, with her grandmother on the outside, then Golda, their mother and father, and then their grandmother.

The next time she visited her grandmother she walked over to the shelf and touched the dolls. Her *Bubbe* watched her, with tired eyes, but didn't say anything. She opened up the one full of her treasures and took four of the tiny pieces of paper. If she noticed, she didn't say anything.

That night, Kayla finished each piece. She worried if each face had enough detail, if they looked real, if they fit inside each other properly. After she fired them on a small kiln near her house, she brought them home, and put a note in each of their mouths.

The next morning, she woke up to find her figurines smashed to pieces, the pieces of paper crumpled all around them.

She staggered into her hallway, where she heard a competing chorus of voices coming from her kitchen.

An older woman turned her head away from the stove and smiled at her.

There was something about her nose, and her cheekbones, the intensity of her eyebrows that was so familiar.

Kayla squinted. "Golda?"

Golda's chest shook with laughter. "Of course, *maidele*, who were you expecting, the queen?"

A woman her mother's age, and a girl her age blinked back at her from her glass Ikea table.

The girl couldn't quite pass as her sister but there was a definite family resemblance.

"Frida, get your cousin a glass of water. Kaylaleh, have you been drinking again?"

Kayla was about to answer when she heard her phone ring.

She padded back to her bedroom and answered. "I knew you could do it," her *Bubbe* said without even saying hello first. Her laughter rang out clear and unguarded.

Proteksiye and Mazel

FOR DAYS I'd been having nightmares that kept my whole family awake. I'd scream and everyone would take turns trying to soothe me. Sometimes I'd see my brother roll his big blue eyes, my mother shushing him, while she stroked my long, knotted curls. I had the same hair as hers, but mine was a lighter brown and hers was smoother and softer. Somehow even now, she smelled vaguely of lavender and talcum powder. Sometimes I'd feel my brother's hand on my back.

I had a reoccurring dream about our neighbourhood catching fire, all the buildings, all the people inside, even people in hiding went up in flames. I could feel the hot air rising around me, the heat licking the bottoms of my feet, knowing it was over for me.

I never understood how my brother and sister could see the shaky handed, hollow- eyed hunger of former friends and acquaintances and hear the rumours every day and still believe that we'd survive and life would go back to normal one day if we stayed here.

My dad's close relationship with the *Altestenrat* had gotten us easier work assignments, in the good workshops, which was what really mattered, because if we could work, we could stay, but still.

My brother could step over a dead body on the street and magically erase it from his mind. It was a rolled -up carpet, it was a coffee table missing a leg, it was a pile of wood for kindling.

Sometimes when we walked on the street together, I'd see his nose tense, his eyes taking in the sight of someone we'd known once, a friend from school, a neighbour, now just a body, the air full of rot and his cigarette smoke.

He'd cover my eyes with one hand, lead me away with the other, a cigarette dangling from his lips. In another life, he'd be in Paris, studying with the great Jewish artists like Soutine. He was always talking about Soutine, and Chagall, even Picasso.

My brother believed in our father and his influence. "We have *protektsiye*, Adasye," he'd say. "We've got *mazel*."

I was less confident but I kept it to myself.

My brother was a genius who could read when he was three. He could draw and write beautifully and do math and if we'd been a more religious family he would've gone to the Slobodka Yeshiva, at least that's what our religious grandfather used to say. I wanted so badly to believe anything he said, the way I used to when we were younger. I used to pull his arm, and say "*zag mir, Iliyash*," and he'd tell me what our parents were talking about or what was going to happen.

The running joke in our family when I was little was at my age, Ilya could count to a million, Chaya could count to the hundreds of thousands, and I could count to thirteen. I didn't have the brains for math. Or school. I was so happy when they forced us to stop going. I didn't even want to go to the underground schools that the teachers set up illegally in the ghetto.

When I was little, I played soccer and swam with the boys, climbed trees and came home dirty, twigs in my hair, dirt embedded on the soles of my feet.

My sister, like Ilya could put a positive face on anything. She got married in this place, and to a man my family would not normally have approved of. My dad bribed the council and some smugglers to bring in sugar and flour for cake, alcohol, and cigarettes.

People danced, my sister draped in white, her cheeks flushed red, beads of sweat like pearls gathering at her hairline. They moved into the apartment next door, sharing it with one other couple.

My brother managed to always have the connections for parties, dancing, and good times, even in our otherwise hermetically sealed life. When he had no work, or school, he walked around smoking, talking to girls, feeling like a flâneur, he said. I didn't know what a flâneur was, and I was too embarrassed to ask, but I pictured him, in fine silks and velvets, books tucked under his arms, strolling around like a young emperor, everyone knowing how important he was and stopping to talk to him. It was the life he would have had, if we were living somewhere else.

Our favourite part of the ghetto was the beach, a small strip of rocks and sand along the banks of the Vilija river.

Ilya elbowed me the first time we went together. "Look at this, Adaske. We're all here, half naked and enjoying ourselves, no armbands with stars of David, no people with privileges, or people without, just all of *amcho*."

Some days, the beach was covered with revellers. There was hardly an inch of sand or dirt or even water that wasn't packed. There weren't as many kids as there used to be, but the ones that had been hidden, in closets or in the hospital were taken by nurses of friends of their mothers. They'd splash in the water, laughing for the first time, sounding like real kids. We saw adults of all ages revelling in the moment or in old memories. We saw tensions loosen, people actually hoping for a future after all of this.

The boys, including Ilya, had dates there, girls with long hair and dresses with fraying edges, looking at him with hungry eyes, trying to take in his heady optimism. I don't know what he promised them, a good life in another city or country, or just the chance to be his love and his muse. I wondered if he wrote them poetry.

I kept to myself, mostly. I was afraid to get close to someone I'd never see again.

His friend Dovid walked me home one afternoon. He smelled like cool air and sweat, turnips and leftover onion. We talked a lot, but I hardly heard him, I was so consumed with the thought of us being alone. "How old are you now, Daske?" he asked me when we got to my building. "Sixteen," I mumbled, and I felt him kiss my cheek. His lips were dry and soft, like tissue paper, and butterfly wings. I felt the heat rising in my face, but I didn't tell anyone.

My brother said we should go to the beach as much as we could now because soon they'd stop us. The Jewish police managed to cross had easily crossed over to the other side, which was downtown, which made it clear that in. In theory, anyone could escape.

I'm not sure he meant to give me any ideas, but it planted a seed.

The water was a refreshing, biting cold. I was a decent swimmer, and I started to practice whenever I could, trying to swim as far as I could, as fast as I could.

One night I dreamed I was walking alone through a museum. Each room had a shiny, maroon door, and when I opened it, they were full of photo exhibits. I edged into a room full of wall- sized photos of Kovno, staring at my family's apartment building, our neighbour's houses, our street, our bakery, our synagogue. There were photos of the ghetto. There was one of my father and the rest of the ghetto police, then another of the five members of *Alstenrat*, wearing suits like they were coming from a board meeting, standing tall. There were photos of families at the beach, my sister smiling shyly at the camera in one of them, hiding behind her husband as the water pooled around their toes. A few photos down, in his own small portrait, was Ilya. He was sitting on the ground, scribbling something into his notebook, his dark eyebrows furrowed like he was trying to find the right word.

A woman with blond hair slicked back into a bun, with lipstick that matched the door asked in a German accent if I thought the exhibit was interesting. She was wearing large diamond earrings that shone like chandeliers.

"It's interesting," she said, "to learn about the people who used to live here, isn't it?"

Her earrings looked just like the ones our neighbour Mrs. Cohen used to wear with her mink collared jacket when she went to the opera with her husband. The Cohens were old and were in one of the first groups sent to the Fort.

I want to rip the earrings out of her tiny, shell pink ears. Why aren't you more afraid of me, I thought.

Can't you see I'm one of them, I tried to ask her, but my mouth wouldn't move.

I felt my legs kick, then I heard myself yelling, in real life, loud enough to wake my parents.

I knew it was time to try to swim all the way to the other side. I never let myself think about drowning. When your life depends on something, you don't have time to think about whether or not it's safe.

I never thought about whether I was crazy, or what would happen if my instincts proved to be right.

The only person I could bring myself to tell was my mother. She cried and made me promise not to tell my father. She gave me a little bit of money and helped me sew it into the lining of my dress. She told me about a farmer she treated for very little when she was a dental assistant before the war. She drew a map to his farm.

"You're a practical girl," she said to me, holding my shoulders, looking me in the eye.

"You do whatever you need to do to survive."

I begged her to come with me, but she shook her head and sighed.

I tried to memorize her high cheekbones, the lines around her mouth, the slight widow's peak on her forehead when she leaned down to kiss me. Her grip was strong.

After curfew I walked down to the beach, ducking into alleys at the slightest noise, convinced I was hearing soldiers.

By the time I got there it was too dark to see anything, but the water lapped comfortingly around my ankles.

I took off my shoes, and put my sweater, jacket, and the food my mother had given me in a bag that I tied to the top of my shoulders.

I glided in carefully, as quietly as I could. I tried to keep my arms as close to the surface as possible to keep my bag dry.

It was almost 5:00 am. I was half asleep, swimming and dreaming that it was my birthday and my mom had somehow procured me a giant, shiny red apple. I took a bite of its sweet juicy texture, and my teeth began to fall out one by one. My mother started giving me a lecture about not taking care of my teeth, and I shake my head, tell her how hard I'm trying, and watch the rest of my teeth fall out. I can't eat it and my brother and sister fight over it, and he wins. I come to, river water flooding my mouth, and I'm almost at the other shore, with the sky lightening above me.

I crawled to the shore, wrung out my hair, shook out my bag. I took out my soaked jacket, wrapped it around myself. I registered the cold for the first time, but I'd made it and it was still dark enough to keep hiding.

Exhilarated, I ripped my Star of David off, dug a hole and buried it as deeply as I could.

I hid in passageways, and alleys, walking and half starving until I got to a forest, full of oak and linden trees. I thought I was dreaming when I heard Yiddish, but it turned out one of the voices was Jacob's, a friend of Ilya's who'd escaped the ghetto after the first big *Aktion*.

He put his hand on my shoulder, looked me in the eye and asked quietly if Ilya was planning to escape too. I shook my head and looked away.

Two days later, I got a ride to the farmer's house.

I slept in a hidden bunker under his barn, with straw and blankets. Sometimes late at night they let me come out and walk around. We were miles from the next farm, but we were all still nervous. His wife fed me and helped me when I got lice.

I got one letter from my mom three months later. She addressed me by my full name, Hadasa, which no one ever did. She said I had to live up to my name now, hide my identity like Queen Esther, for the sake of other Jews. She wrote that she loved me and had faith that I would get there safely. She gave me instructions for the farmer, Edgaras on which smuggler to contact to get more money. He never took me up on it.

In the envelope my mother had tucked a small, folded sketch of Ilya and me at the beach. I could hear the water, and his dry laugh as I looked at it. In his tiny, curving print, he'd written in the bottom left corner: "*Mir benken dikh shvester.*" We miss you, sister.

I kept it under my pillow for years.

Blasting Molly Rockets

WHEN SHE WOKE UP in the doorway, the rusting metal felt cold against her cheek, like an ice pack against a slowly puffing bruise. It almost made her miss her mother, for a second.

Sometimes she slept on couches, and she was starting to see someone, another musician of course, a drummer this time, but she wasn't the kind of girl who fucked for a clean pillowcase, a milk crate full of vinyl and a wobbly Ikea bookshelf stuffed with Scandinavian philosophers.

She shook out her long thick hair, registered the dust on her olive-green cargo pants, the smell of sweat barely covered by her amber roll-on perfume. The rips she tore herself, the dirt, the hand sown patches of punk bands, the extra streak of dust above her right eyebrow were all good for her image. She ran two fingers through her bangs.

She took out a small compact from her pocket. It was slightly cracked and the corners had the white, chalky residue of leftover coke. So did the keys she'd accidentally kept from her parents' front door.

The thought of having keys but spending endless nights sleeping in dirty *bandos* or on random friend of friends couches and occasionally, in the doorway of the store she worked in, made her laugh. It came out a little hoarse, but it was there.

She took out the bright red lipstick from her pocket.

She had big, floppy lips, everyone always said so, and at first she was convinced that the glossy, ruby shade made her look like she was starring in a clown porn. But everyone convinced her that it looked badass and now she hardly recognized herself without it.

She heard the manager, Stuart, shuffling in awkwardly behind her, his red lumberjacket brushing up against her hand. She took out her pack of cigarettes and offered him one. At least twice a day they stood outside in the alleyway, smoking together. He smelled like hair gel and the Kiehl's moisturizer his girlfriend used, mixed with weed.

He put his arm around her.

"Moll, I'm worried about you. It's going to start snowing soon …"

He looked down awkwardly at his callused hands.

They were all musicians working at a second-hand clothing store that sold band T-shirts to people who were born thirty or forty years after the bands' heyday.

He dropped his voice lower. "You can always stay with us if you need to."

She laughed, the gap between her front teeth snagging the bottom of her lips.

"I'm okay, Stu," she said. She hadn't been planning to tell him, but it came out. "I just signed a deal. They're going to pay my rent and pay for studio time."

His brown eyes bulged like a lemur's but he didn't say anything. His sweet silence reminded her of her little brother's. She steadied herself on his arm, took out her cheap burner phone and showed him the photo of the contract, her signature looping but messy, like she hadn't been practicing it for years.

He stared at her and looked away.

"Do you ever think about why these creepy old men give you these once in a lifetime chances, while the rest of us who've been at it longer than you are still struggling?"

She gave him a shove.

"No," she answered. But sometimes late night she did wonder.

She knew they signed her because of her killer live presence. Days before, she'd played them some songs, jumped from guitar to keys to drums. Later, when her band showed up, she shook out her hair, screamed out certain lines, the drug ones, the fuck you ones, her fingers shredding on her borrowed electric guitar. She jumped on the table, knocked Suit Jacket's glass of Jack onto the floor. The glass broke in perfect rhythm, like it was planned.

* * *

The first thing she did in her new apartment was soak in a bath. She showered when she crashed on friend's couches, but she was never alone, never free to use all the hot water, as many products as she wanted.

They gave her money, the man in the blue jeans and soft suit jacket, who reminded her of one of her uncles, and the female VP, who was fine boned with long, sharp red nails that she told her were almond shaped.

They didn't want her living so rough. They believed in her.

The thought made her giddy.

She took the money they gave her, bought bath bombs, shampoo and conditioner. She tried to decide what to listen to. She settled on a mix of Metallica and Hole, Sonic Youth and Dinosaur Jr. The drummer brought over the good stuff, Spanish red wine, and some black tar, shiny like onyx, sticky as honey. "That must have been expensive," she said after she kissed him.

"What are you talking about?" He answered too slowly, too loudly. "We're celebrating."

* * *

It wasn't boys who got her into drugs. It was about being as big and as loud and as flashy and as much of a legend as you dreamed you could be. When she heard that Marianne Faithfull got into heroin after reading *Naked Lunch*, it made total sense.

If from the time you're little, tons of people tell you you're a weirdo, you believe it, and it's only when you reach adulthood that you realize it might be okay. She was luckier than most, she knew. The things that people ridiculed her for were what her audience celebrated her for now.

Her band's name, Blasting Molly Rockets, came from the rich little girls who wouldn't let her play with their Polly Pockets.

When you're thirteen you start getting into Oxys, and Percs and eventually Fentanyl, when you lose your virginity when your parents find you watching porn with and kissing your female best friend when you're fourteen, and they make you get rid of all your music and tear the door torn off your bedroom so they can watch you at all times, you decide to lean in.

She loved being on stage, her long, full hair framing her face like a lioness, dancing on bars, trashing stages, while people danced and screamed and touched a little bit of freedom for the first time.

The other day, she was taking the subway, and a girl who looked fourteen, in a ripped T-shirt full of punk buttons and safety pins and clumpy knotted brown hair, told her she saw her play at an all age's show two weeks before. She was from the suburbs too, and she was learning how to play guitar. The girl's hands shook as they took a selfie.

They say when you get what it never feels as good as you imagined, but sometimes it does. For a moment, it felt okay that her parents never called. It felt okay that she'd never be the person they wanted her to be. In that moment everything she was doing felt like enough. She'd spend the rest of her life trying to hold on to that feeling.

Always An Angel, Never A God

Always an angel/never a God/
I don't know why I am the way I am.
—Boygenius, Not Strong Enough

I USED TO TELL PEOPLE I was a crack baby. It's not exactly true but it's not entirely untrue either. They'd either blink at me in shock, raise an eyebrow slowly like sorry, what? Or they'd laugh. I always liked the ones who laughed, the more the better. If nothing else, I've always been an entertainer.

People used to look at me like I'd led an extraordinary life. They'd ask me questions about my past, like how partying and being self destructive inform my art. They'd ask me if I consider myself a nepo baby, if I think I deserve the things I have.

The truth is, does anyone? If you're born white, speaking English in America, you have advantages that a lot of people don't have.

If you had parents who were famous, a mom who was a model and a muse to many a notorious, sleazy guitarist, and a dad who bounced around had lots of kids but still managed somehow to be a respected actor, you have it better than most. I'd never argue with that.

But if you think you wouldn't have done exactly what I did if you were in my situation, you're kidding yourself.

It all started with the intoxicating windfall of getting paid to stand around in fancy underwear. A few hours of posing, money deposited straight into your bank account. If you're fourteen, and you've never had a job, thousands can feel like millions, your parents stepping out of the shadows for the first time, saying they're proud, your dad springing for an apartment, your mom paying for a full-time housekeeper to help you keep track of things.

I wasn't tall, so I couldn't do runway, but I could do print, all those ads of underage-looking girls, suggesting sex, selling you unisex perfume, oversized jean jackets, and tiny, white cotton undies.

Editors and photographers told me that my weird looks were charming. "Look at the way her eye teeth stick out, she's a regular girl next door. Look at her messy waves, like she just came back from surfing. Look at her full lips, and her porcelain skin, she looks like a doll."

They liked it when they could see my clavicles, my hip bones, they liked it when my cheekbones stood out.

It was a small price to pay.

It was like living in my own hotel room, the bed sheets made with stiff hospital corners, the toilet paper folded down into triangles, a fridge stocked with food I'd never eat. What I remember most of all is the decadence, the constant clacking of friends' stilettos, cute shaggy boy actors I lost my virginity and any sense of urgency to, and drugs that felt like my mama's full lips pressed warmly against my forehead. I could give you the usual BS about drugs and genetics, I could say I was addicted to heroin in utero, and it was a matter of time before I'd wanted it again, but it was even simpler than that; felt amazing until it didn't. I danced at clubs when I was underage, and I had socialite friends, and did all the drugs, China White, Black Tar, Molly, and I drank tons. But after a while, I was throwing up and forgetting to eat, getting sentimental when I went to movies, crying on swings. My parents agreed to send me to rehab, where I tried to take it seriously, even though I knew I was different from them.

I lived in lots of different houses growing up. When my parents were together, we lived in a big house. The windows were always covered, and in the mornings, when the sun streamed in, there were half dressed adults sprawled out all over the floors and beds, like a disquieting Delacroix painting. My dad went to jail for drug trafficking, and later, when I was five, and accidentally drank a cup of his mescaline tea, and almost died, he went to jail for trying to kidnap me.

I have movie still memories, coated in candy floss clouds, of chasing my little sister around a field of high grass and dandelions. We were wearing white dresses and black rainboots, playing in mud, chasing, making daisy crowns. I think it happened, but there are no photos.

There are no pictures of the day the courts decided my parents were both unfit and made my sister and I live with different foster parents. There are some photos of happier days, sharing a room with my foster sister, collecting stickers, having the family golden retriever, Rosie sleeping with me on my bed. There were no pictures of the tears I cried after three years when they told me I had to leave and get shunted again between my mom's house and my dad's. I'd watch my mom drink late at night, the lines around her mouth looking more pronounced. I'd tell her she was beautiful, sometimes I'd sing to her. She was always impossibly glamorous, especially when she was so tired she was vulnerable and open. She kept her hair long my whole life, it was always perfectly dyed, long blond waves, and when she fell asleep she looked like an angel.

I never thought I'd want to be a mom or even a wife after everything I went through. To want to have a family, you have to be willing to give up everything you've ever wanted for someone else. I bet you to some people that seems like nothing, but to me it was unimaginable, to belong to a group of people you'd do anything for, to love so fiercely you could kill for them.

I never wanted it until I met Rich. We met at a house party. I liked him because unlike most of the guys there, he didn't hit on me. His eyes were bright chips of sky. He had a dimple in his chin and soft wavy dark hair that smelled like mangoes. He moved like he was comfortable in his own skin. When I said I liked his striped, brown shirt he laughed and said he had no idea where he'd gotten it but it was probably cheap and vintage.

When we talked about songs he started humming and singing, curling his right fist into a microphone, drumming on his thighs. We found our way into the guy's library and had a conversation about Cormac McCarthy and Hunter S. Thompson and it was nice, just talking about books. He didn't fit in, but he moved so naturally, like the world and this mansion full of much more famous people were all his. When he kissed me, his lips were thin, and he tasted like a mixture of mint gum and tobacco but I was intoxicated. Before long, he was all I could think about. He made me chase him, which was something I'd never had to do, but it made me feel oddly in control, like I was choosing him and us, not just waiting for something to happen to me.

It wasn't long before we were living together.

"You've worked so hard since you were really young," he said, "You've seen too much."

So for the first time in years, I did nothing. I gardened and drew and wrote and cooked. It was weird at first, but then it felt wonderful. He asked me to marry him, and we got married in a castle in Italy, with all of our friends, and friends of friends. I found myself pregnant twice, with two blonde little girls, just a year and a half apart, like me and my sister. I had natural births, no drugs for me or us again, ever, while Richie played guitar softly in the background and told me how amazing and powerful I was. We were one of those families you read about or watch on a cheesy sitcom, living in a beautiful, clean house, playing and laughing and listening to music. He dragged me to his church on Sundays, and even though the media was always demonising them, I was happy there. It gave my life structure and meaning.

I never thought I could experience a love like that, the kind that Poe wrote about, a love that was more than love.

So when those girls from years before I even met him came after him, I didn't have a choice. When their hateful words starting hitting the tabloids, he started losing work. His record label and management dropped him. I had to tell them to fuck off, I had to show them everything they would destroy if they kept telling these lies about him. I pretended to be on their side when everything started. I pretended to want to hear them. I talked about #MeToo and #TimesUp and I said all the right things. Then eventually, I got to the truth; they were nothing more than gold diggers trying to extort an innocent man. No one was going to believe them, and if anyone did, it was his two baby daughter's lives who would hang in the balance.

Two of them walked away, but three of them didn't. I started small scale at first, delivering LIAR banners to the places they worked, hacking their social media where I told everyone they were fame whores, convincing some of their friends that they were crazy.

When the case went to trial, I clung to Rich. I was his anchor, I believed him. At night, we cried about the trauma and sleepless nights it caused us.

I really never believed that he'd be found guilty.

I stopped hearing the judge after the first count.

It's not true that it happened that day in the court. There are photos to prove it, and still people lie to make the story sound better. I was eating a kale salad at a restaurant near the courthouse two days later. One of the musicians who won, the toughest of all, Wendy Sullivan, came right up to me. She was almost in my face, but her eyes were full of pity.

"Gemma Rae," she said quietly. "I'm so relieved it happened, but I do feel for you and Jade and Pearl."

Something about hearing my babies' names come out of her mouth brought on a visceral reaction. I don't remember doing it to be honest. I felt myself raise my hands, I thought of my mom, who always wanted me to eat everything with a knife and fork, all elegant and I stood up, holding them up to her.

The next thing I remember is her scream, the blood coming out of her neck and forehead.

Everyone knows she survived, a double victim now, she was all anyone was worried about.

Our lawyer tried to argue about my mental state, the trauma of my husband being in jail, the trauma of my childhood, my kids going back into foster care.

I got my sentence reduced, but I remain here, in a different building than Rich, hoping he'll want me when all of this is over. I still love him and my girls as much as ever.

I hope one day they'll understand me.

All the Lives that Could Have Been

IT HAD BEEN A FEW YEARS since I'd been home, and I'd intentionally kept the visit short. I was there for Passover, for nine days, one before and the eight days of the holiday after, and not a day longer. I wasn't avoiding anything, as much as I was trying consciously to create distance.

I loved the town I grew up in, in a way that had never been cool to admit. I love that everything always stays the same. I walk its main street in my head on nights when anxiety keeps me awake, when I can't slow the thoughts or the feelings down until I picture my favourite restaurants and coffee shop, my favourite used bookstore, the terrible pizzeria, the semi decent one, the useless drug store that never seems to have anything, the newer, fancier one, the bakery, the seamstress, all the other buildings, the elementary school, my apartment building.

When you grow up in a place with only two high schools, you know everyone your own age, or a year or two older or younger, give or take. Danny, the guy who runs the bakery on our street, knew my grandmother, tells me he misses her since she passed way. The Seder, I knew would seem strange without her effusive compliments, without the money she'd stuff into all of her grandchildren's pockets on our way out.

Hadar, the neighbour who owns the white rescue dog, Bobby, whose ears were cruelly cut in half, runs over to say hi, asks about my rescue dogs.

"They're good," I say, "aside from the Canadian winter."

I don't tell her how the one lives for the snow, how he revels in it, rolls in it, would fall asleep in a pile of it if I didn't force him to come inside. I don't tell her that I don't have to take him to groomers to get him ridiculous lion style hair cuts anymore. He looks majestic now. His tail looks like a fountain.

I don't tell her how much I miss the heat, how I take vitamin D and have a special lamp on my desk that makes me feel like a baby in an incubator. I don't tell how much I miss everyone's small talk, everyone acting like an extra set of parents, or relatives, telling me what to do. Canadians are far too polite for that, I want to tell her. I never thought I'd miss all the unsolicited advice.

She hugs me.

"We miss you, Shira'le," she says. "You should try to visit more often."

When my parents moved us to Canada, they kept the apartment in case one of us wanted to move back. We all took turns here, my sister, and my brother and I, but we all ended up back in Montreal.

I schedule my days so I'm seeing multiple friends and relatives. On my last day, I see my friend Natalia. She's a brilliant writer who speaks Russian and English and Hebrew, who reads the classics in their original languages. She has Spina Bifida, and says she taught herself English on the many days she spent at home, too sick to go to school. Through a surrogate, she and her husband had twin babies. I visit them loaded with gifts. We take photos and I find myself teary when I leave.

On my way out, I walk past the store Adar manages. I think of my David, the house we lived in in Côte St-Luc, our dogs.

I know Adar lives with a woman. When we ran into each other a few years back, when it was new. He said it was the best relationship he'd ever been in, and it felt like he'd snapped a thick elastic band across my cheek. I bragged to him about David, his wealthy parents and their fancy mansion which they called a cottage in the Laurentians, all the ski trips. He looked at me like he couldn't decide if I'd lost my mind, if he'd ever really known me, and he choked out, "As long as you're happy," and I said I was. I made it sound like we were about to get engaged, even though he'd only recently asked me to be his girlfriend. We hadn't talked since.

A few steps down, Adar sees me through the giant glass windows, waves me over.

His smile is pure sunshine, his dishwater blonde hair pulled up in a messy man bun, his skin only lightly freckled despite the heat.

"You look good," I found myself saying, and he grinned as if I was telling him I still loved him. You look the same is what I meant, and it's comforting, but I kept my mouth shut.

I wasn't effusive enough when we were together. He once told me that I only told him I loved him after we broke up. I wanted to be more generous now.

I was pregnant and in my second trimester. Certain outfits hid it better, my peasant shirts, my loose dresses, but the skirt I was wearing showed too much.

I saw his eyes travelling across my body.

"Wow," he said, and looked away. "Did I tell you that my wife is pregnant too?"

I wasn't sure which detail cut most.

"When did you get married?"

He snorted. "I didn't. I never want to get married."

"I remember," I said, thinking about the fights we'd had. It was oddly reassuring.

"But she's pregnant now, so people tell me I can't just call her my girlfriend."

He sighed and looked away from me.

"What happens," he asked, "when you finally get something you've always wanted?"

When we were in our twenties I knew he wanted kids. He talked about taking kids on camping trips, showing them the beauty of the ocean. We both had low paying jobs. Neither of us knew what we wanted to do with our lives, but that didn't bother him.

"I didn't know you were so superficial," he yelled at me once.

But is it superficial to want to be comfortable, to want to feel safe, to want a stable life?

"Stability is an illusion," he answered and I wanted to scream but I kicked a dent in his bedroom door and drove home instead.

I knew I could be myself around him on our first date. It felt like I'd been under water for years, choking and sputtering and slowly making my way up to the surface, and he handed me a snorkel and then a scuba tank and I could breathe and stay and explore as much as I wanted to. He made me feel safe. I loved that he rescued dogs and cats off the street. I loved the way his face lit up when he saw me, the way his neighbour said he'd never seen him smile like that. I loved how comfortable he was in his own skin, the way he took everything in stride. It was advice that my grandmother was always giving me. "You've got to learn to take things in stride, Shira," she was always saying, and she liked that he was a calming presence, but she worried about our future.

"You have to look out for yourself in this world," she told me once, waving a candy apple red manicured finger.

I visited home again a year later. I texted him and he told me to meet him at work. We'd been in touch, sporadically, and I thought we were friends now. I thought he might invite me to his house.

He looked worn out in a way that I hadn't seen before, and it looked like more than the exhaustion of early parenthood. He looked miserable.

We showed each other pictures of our babies.

He winced when he saw mine. "He looks just like his father," he said, and I didn't know what to say, so I told him that his daughter was beautiful.

I asked him if they were planning to have more kids, and he shook his head.

"She's in her forties," he said, looked away. "She's older than me."

"So," I said. "Lots of women have babies in their forties …"

He cut me off. "She doesn't want to." And then said: "If I'd known how great it was to be a father, I'd have wanted to have kids with my last girlfriend." He laughed mirthlessly.

"I wish I'd been ready then," I said quietly. All the possibilities washed over me. The places we could have lived, the jobs we could have had.

All the lives that could've been.

Would I have felt trapped, or would we have somehow worked it out? Did I spare myself pain, or did I miss out on the best thing that could have happened to me?

I wondered what would happen if I still lived there, if I showed up all the time, if I wore him down until he couldn't turn me away. I'd done it before, after the first time we broke up. It hadn't taken that much, just consistency.

Maybe I could be the person he deserved now, the one who said I love you everyday, the one who fearlessly said it first, the one who would always be there, no matter what we fought about, the one who held him at night when he was having nightmares, the one who got up to get him water at 5 am, who walked the dogs if they needed it then too, the one who organized everything.

I wondered if we could merge who we were then with all we were now. If I could love his daughter, if he could love my son.

He shook his head at me, his sea green eyes full of everything I was feeling too.

"I don't think so," he answered, even though I hadn't actually asked anything.

I pulled back, trying to take a mental photo of his expression, the tension in his forehead, the downturn of his lips, the softness in his eyes.

We promised each other we'd stay in touch but this time I wasn't sure if we were lying. It wasn't enough, but I told myself that at least it was something.

From the Belly of the Whale

I GAVE A TALK at a synagogue today. The building was the colour of milky Earl Grey, the clouds as heavy as tea bags. I could feel the moisture pooling in my knees and hips. They wanted me and two others, a woman from Poland and a man from Slovakia, to give a talk about our experiences in the war. I was the first one there, dressed down in a blue dress shirt and slacks.

I reached for one of the free black satin yarmulkes and placed it awkwardly on my head before walking over to the stage and taking my seat. For years, I refused to talk about any of it, in public or in private, but recently, I've started agreeing to it sometimes.

I stopped by at my son and daughter in law's house after. They live two streets away, only about a seven-minute walk. They've been having problems with their oldest kid, my grandson, Benji. He had insomnia and night terrors, screaming at the top of his lungs, sleep walking, and now, they said, he was starting to get into trouble at school.

Benji was lying on his bed, comic books spread out everywhere, staring up at his ceiling which was covered in stickers of the planets that were starting to peel off.

I sat down at the chair at his desk, staring up at his school books on the shelf above me, workbooks, science, math, books of Torah.

He asked me what I talked about tonight, and I offered to tell him, if he was sure it wouldn't make his problems worse.

He laughed and said I should go ahead.

"I grew up in a home where everyone was proud to be what we were. My father was an accountant and my mother taught literature. My dad's parents died before I was born and my mom's parents were more religious than us, but we were all proud to be Jewish.

"My Zaidy once said it was our job to be a light unto the nations, so it made sense to me that we had to wear a bright golden star, to remind everyone.

"I was proud when they told me I was old enough to wear it, to watch my mother sew it onto my jacket pocket with careful precision.

"Then one day my Zaidy vanished. He'd refused to shave his beard and was found outside a few minutes after curfew. We never saw him again.

"My parents always loved nature, and one night they took us on an adventure in the woods behind our house. We packed some food and wore our warmest clothes even though it was spring. My mother peeled off our stars and my father dug a deep hole and buried them. My sister and I left a small trail of breadcrumbs behind us at first, so we could find our way home, but our mother picked them all up. We didn't want to get caught by the witch and end up burning in the ovens.

"It was safer to disappear.

"My father had a farmer friend who owned a small store and over time let him and his friends build a bunker underneath.

"We walked into one of his barns, inched down a thin, narrow hole.

"The earth yawned and we climbed down into its dark, giant mouth. It was impossible to see much, aside from a small blow hole at the back, the shape of a pair of tonsils. I could feel the cool air, see patches of light and the feet of passersby, but I knew if I found my way outside I'd be swallowed whole, like my namesake Jonah.

"It was dusty, and the floor was a mix of wooden planks and soil. Still, compared to where we'd lived before, we felt warm and safe.

"My sister and I called it the Cave.

"A big rat we saw on our first night became the White Rabbit. We followed him to a small bent twig we called the key, and pretended it led us to a beautiful garden. We could feel the freshly cut grass under our feet, see the yellow tulips and smell the roses. When we drank our water ration, sometimes it made us grow so tall our heads touched the ceiling or made us shrink so much we could ride on the White Rabbit's back.

"The wooden planks under our feet felt rough, like a cat's tongue, and we used them to set up makeshift beds, but the soil felt soft and velvety. The farmer's wife had given us a blanket, and we spread it on top of the soil, and pretended it was the magic carpet in a *Thousand and One Nights*. We could fly into the night, feel the fresh air, see the glittering stars and coloured lights below that shone like candies. We could fly out in the daytime, see the kids playing soccer in the green field, fly our carpet down and I could join in, my limbs vibrating, giddy in anticipation.

"The farmer's wife would bring us potatoes and bread.

"My mom would drill us in the alphabet. She'd trace the letters and the sounds in my palms and as fast as we could, we'd tell her all the answers. My Bubbe would drill us on the rules of Shabbat, the Jewish calendar, what holiday was coming next.

"We had lice and my mom told us about a story called "Leiningen Versus the Ants." We had to catch the lice and squash them. We had to count to ten and see how many we could get. 'We have to get them before they hurt us,' she would say, and we'd try our hardest to pick them off the fastest.

"One night, we heard the farmer get arrested and we knew we had to escape. We went back to the forest, opening our mouths as wide as possible to drink the fresh, cool air. Our knees buckled but we kept walking.

"Along the way, we found one of our uncles, and he uncovered another hiding place for us, this time in an attic, with another family. It smelled like sweat and fear, and we had to be much quieter, but we were only there for two months until we were liberated.

"It felt like being vomited from the whale's belly, being squeezed against its intestines and its throat, feeling its heart pound as we slowly pushed our heads out, one by one.

"First glitter and gum and cigarettes were rained on us by the soldiers. They fed us and checked us for diseases and found us places to stay.

"Then the shadows came back. People who were living in our house were sorry that we survived.

"My mom died not long after that.

"It took a few years, but eventually the rest of us came to Canada. For a long time I hid, like the original Jonah, from being Jewish. It had only ever caused my family problems. When people asked me what it was like to be a survivor, I told them I was a kid, I didn't remember anything.

But eventually, it caught up with me. It wasn't a question of what I believed, just a statement of who I was, and if I denied it, I realized I was hurting myself."

I was speaking loudly, I realized, but when I looked over at Benji, I found that he was asleep.

I gently covered him up to his chin, whispered a prayer about the angels protecting him, like my Zadie used to sing to me, and quietly turned out his light.

Like an Alligator Eyeing a Small Fish

NO ONE EVER REALLY intends to end it all. I mean, of course, people flirt with death. People entertain the possibility if they're feeling shitty, maybe they imagine their own life without them, people's deep regrets or total indifference.

I'd thought about all of these things, of course. Anyone who uses does.

It doesn't matter how you do it, if you pop an Adderall or three just to get you through your classes and your part time job, if you need Oxys or Ambien to chill the fuck out afterwards, if you fall into a K-hole with friends on the weekend, staring at all the beauty all around you, tapping and chewing ASMR style, if you keep a syringe of Fentanyl in your Uggs for the perfect moment, that thick blue vein running over the fleshy part of your foot, just before your toes, a delicious thrill running through you as you contemplate it.

The problem is one drug necessitates another. But when you beat the odds a certain number of times you start to feel superhuman. Built for both relaxation and destruction. That's what I believed on the day it happened. I was at this guy Craig's house, sitting on his lap, feeling his kneecaps in my butt bones, and it hurt, so I collapsed into his blue corduroy beanbag chair. It made me laugh because it felt like it belonged in a little boy's room. There was laughter and talking around me, weed and cigarette smoke, some hip hop playing, and it all melted into the background. I closed my eyes and heard that song that my older sister played when I was little, the one where the guy sings "I am for real" and I insisted it was "I am for eels" just to drive Ali nuts. I heard OutKast, and I thought of her and I opened my eyes and I tried to get up but I couldn't. My nails looked blue, just like Ali's when she painted them navy just to piss our mom off. I tried to tell someone but no words came out. I was suddenly cold and tired and my last thought was about being lucky that this was now, not like when it happened to Al and there were no drugs like Naloxone to bring you back. I wondered if I'd see her again, if that's what came next, and I sort of felt relieved that everything had caught up to me finally, and then there was nothing.

* * *

My eyes popped open. None of the usual fluttering and glued together eyelashes from too many days of sleeping in mascara. My face and hair felt smooth, my body got up and moved easily. There was no one around me, and the apartment was quiet and eerily dark. I let myself out and walked out into the hallway, and when I got into the elevator, a short woman in a baby blue cardigan twin set and fitted khakis smiled at me. Her dark hair was back in some kind of fancy chignon. I looked down at my bare knees, popping out of the ripped holes. I probably looked like a dirtbag next to her.

"You must be Jamie."

The cloudy headed, cotton candy mouthed feeling from earlier in the night had faded. It was easier to talk.

"Sorry, have we met before?"

She laughed. "I'm Shelly. I've seen you around."

"You have?"

She nods.

I feel my heart pounding and as we get out of the elevator she hands me something.

It's a folded over note written on a tiny scrap of lined paper, like a half a page in those little notebooks Ali had. Inside is her unmistakably messy writing. *Hi James*, it says, *hope you're behaving and keeping an open mind.* On the back, in her tiny scrawl, it says *I love you.*

I swallow hard and stare ahead of me. The lobby looks less like Craig's and more like the lobby of my grandparents' old apartment building. I half expect it to smell like cholent or herring or to be full of old Orthodox Jews who use the Shabbat elevator every day of the week. It isn't.

Shelley steers me by the elbow past a front desk with two attendants.

"We don't have to sign you in, yet. I'm just going to give you a tour."

She points things out, the gym, the pool, and I want to slow down, look at the groups of people, ask who they are, but she leads me to another elevator. This one is round and made of blue glass.

"I was going to show you where people live, if they choose to live here, although there are other options. It's just, there was a special request from someone here to see you, and I thought we could do that first."

I felt my heart race. "My sister?"

She shook her head. "No, I'm sorry, Jamie. That's not scheduled to happen just yet."

"Then who? My grandfather?"

She shook her head again, her shiny, brown bob bouncing from side to side.

"We understand that you're a writer."

I snorted. "If by a writer you mean the worst creative writing student in my program, sure. One of my professors grabbed one of my poems off my desk, read the first few lines out loud, slammed it down, and said: 'This is shit.' But yeah, sure, I'm a writer." I took a breath.

"You know I took this year off because school has been fucking impossible? I don't have a Plan B. It's not like I could still go to medical school if this writing thing doesn't pan out."

"Jamie," she said gently, "this happens to a lot of people. The person who wants to meet you had no formal writing training, but she became one of the most famous writers in history."

I looked at her incredulously. "And she wants to meet me? Why?"

She gave me a tight smile. "She's very critical of her own work too. She had a feeling you'd have certain things in common. We were, of course, happy to oblige."

"Who is she?"

"She prefers that I not tell you. She'll introduce herself when you get there."

I followed her out of the elevator and into a bright, wide hallway.

We were soon outside a heavy white door.

"She lives in the penthouse," she explained, as we walked into her foyer.

Her living room was full of floor to ceiling books, like the library scene in *Beauty and the Beast*.

She was sitting on a blue leather couch, reading, sinking into the cushions, when she looked up and noticed us. She had intense brown eyes, full brows and delicate features. Her hair was wavy and grey. Her cheeks were lightly dusted with blush.

I looked down at my ratty jeans and navy blue hoodie, wishing I'd asked if I could change.

She got up and gestured to another room.

"Let's talk in my office," she said.

"I'm really sorry, I don't recognize you," I started to say.

She smiled like an alligator eyeing a small fish.

"Annalies," she said, extending a veiny, crepey hand.

"Jamie," I answered, as yet unsure, realizing that I still had no idea who she was.

A Charlotte Saloman painting with the words *Leben Oder Theater, Life or Theatre* stared back at me from the opposite wall. Behind me was what looked like a Matisse.

She sat down at her desk and gestured to a chair in the corner.

"Bring it closer. You most likely know me as Anne."

"Anne ...?"

"Frank, dear."

I exhaled sharply.

In one of my last assignments for school, we were asked to critically analyse a work of Creative Non-Fiction we found highly overrated. I'd chosen her diary. It was one of the books they made us read in school, that everyone thought I'd love because I was Jewish, but it was boring, and in many ways, Anne was unexceptional. I'd compared it unflatteringly to Elie Wiesel's *Night*.

I started to sweat.

"It might interest you to know that I quite liked your essay."

"You what?"

"I agree with you. After all, it wasn't my idea to publish it. Imagine the only piece of writing you have published being something you never wanted anyone to read. I was so humiliated when I found out. Can you imagine? I was in my twenties, and after everything I'd seen and felt and experienced, to hear about people getting excited about my naïve, girlish statements about a crush on a boy and the goodness of humanity? It was too much. And it only got more popular, translated into more languages, people mourning over the loss of my life like they knew me."

"Weren't you being yourself in your diary? Or was it like Instagram, where you only curate your best thoughts?"

She leaned in. "I'll tell you something. Once you write something down, you're shaping it, and changing it. It becomes a story, and stories always contain inaccuracies and fictions. And don't forget, trauma and tragedy change us."

"Change us how?"

"You can't unsee hunger and mass deaths. You can't unsee lice and disease and your sister dying." She paused. "But you know something about that."

I nodded.

"From what I understand, you can't unsee the things you saw in the throes of your addiction either."

I shrugged. Everything I'd lived when I was high had felt unreal and dreamlike.

"It's fine. It's all material. The more you've lived, the more insight you have, well hopefully anyway. What I've written here is ten times better than anything I ever wrote on earth, believe me."

"Can I read something?"

"Of course, of course," she said, gesturing to a bookshelf of her books, and a pile of papers on her desk.

"You don't want to be a writer who is adored for being young and precocious and pure. You want to be admired for being complex and unpredictable. If I could go down to earth, sometimes I think, you know what I'd do? Aside from visiting my father's grave, I'd go visit all those statues of me, you know where they make me look like Joan of Arc, or I'd visit that famous museum they made for me, and I'd tell anyone who would listen that I was just a person. A person who could have done a lot of things, good and bad. A person who never had a chance to get into real trouble in their world, but maybe I would have."

"You seem to have a good life here," I said, looking around.

"I do. You know, my mother is here. And my sister. I was married three times, can you imagine? I had two kids. Some people here, all they want is to be eternally seventeen, or twenty-five. My sister doesn't look a day over forty. Maybe you'll meet her still. But I couldn't remain stagnant. I wanted to grow and change. And I think I have."

She leaned in closely. "A lot of survivors couldn't stay in this world either. It was too bright, full of too much opportunity. My father was one of them. They wanted darkness. They wanted to rest. They would have done anything to make their thoughts disappear."

She reached for my arm and grabbed it. I felt her nails dig into my flesh.

"Don't be like that. Try to embrace every opportunity. Write about every strange thing that I never got to experience. Write about your sister."

I felt her nails pressing deep into my veins.

I closed my eyes. My shoulders shook. I felt myself breathing heavily, while she stood over me.

* * *

When I opened my eyes I was lying down. My arm was hooked up to an IV. It took a few minutes to register that I was in a hospital.

My mom stood beside my bed, pacing and sniffling. I tried to smile at her.

My cousin Lila stood beside her, holding some books. "In case you feel well enough to read something," she said. At the bottom of the pile was *The Diary of Anne Frank*.

They both looked startled when I started laughing.

Happiness Contained in a Single Bite

When my parents said they were becoming snowbirds, I figured they'd choose a place more relaxing than South Beach. The hottest clubs, restaurants and stores, a playground for celebrities and the very wealthy. "But look," my mom says, "there's the Miami ballet, and look, a library, and another museum."

Little girls, like pocket sized dolls, their hair in tight buns, their posture perfect, all sparkles and determination, duffle bags slung over their shoulders, holding their moms' hands as they run across the street, into the studio for lessons.

I've watched from the sidewalk, through the giant store front window, the coordination as eight little girls dip their bodies and bend their knees and point their toes out in unison. I smiled and clapped and two of them curtsied. I was a terrible dancer as a kid. I could never follow instructions, I could never concentrate enough, or get my body to cooperate. My mind was always running off to more interesting places.

I like the boardwalk first thing in the morning, when the sun is breaking through, like tiger's eyes on a disappearing grey satin canvas. If you go early enough, you can watch the homeless people sleep curled into themselves like caterpillars, their faces peaceful and angelic. You can see their eyelashes flutter mid dream, their eyebrows expressive and thoughtful. You can hope that today they'll find the resources they need to become who they used to be, or everything they could still be.

I love the majesty of the ocean when it's not teeming with highlighter yellow bikinis, or bright red thongs, bros laughing on jet skis or tiny planes with signs up above that announce the hottest place to be.

My parents' neighbours tell me not to walk around alone at night. But ever since Marc and I separated, ever since I moved out into the closet-sized room I try to spend as little time as possible in, it's the only way I manage to get any sleep.

Besides, I tell them, I lived in Parkdale.

They shrug at me, former New Yorkers who think all of Canada, including Toronto, is a frozen backwater.

"There isn't much I haven't seen before," I say, which is both true and not true.

I know someone famous is coming out of a hotel because I see their bodyguards, the flash of their hair extensions, their tiny shorts. In the Walgreens, at 1 am one night, I see the runner up from the current season of the *Voice*, and I tell him I'm a fan, and he looks at me incredulously, like even he doesn't feel that way about himself.

There are giant, hot pink Lucite snails in the park, an installation left over from Art Basel. I think back to art school, when installations were trendy and we were told over and over to write thought provoking artist statements so that everyone could tell the work had meaning.

Half a block further down, next to another expensive hotel is a ceramic Hello Kitty fountain. I'd thought it was part of the art show too, I imagined the statement, an unabashed homage to youth and kitsch, but apparently it was permanently there, a fixture of the hotel.

I picture the hotelier's young daughter, an anti-Eloise with dark hair and permanently crossed arms who won't visit her dad unless he puts in something especially for her. A trip to Japan that she took with her dad when she was five is her happiest childhood memory.

I picture her sitting beside the fountain, tossing pennies in, wishing for things that seem so simple, that the girl she likes will like her back, and not just as a friend, that she'll be able to come out to him one day, and that he'll still love her, that she'll find Umeboshi plums as good as the ones she had in Japan, the tangy sour salty flavour, the soft melting peel, the giddy feeling of happiness contained in a single bite.

A thin man with tanned skin and greying beard is walking a Chihuahua and a Samoyed, a study in opposites, one tiny, one large, one with glossy, fine fur, the other a walking stuffed animal that actually smiled as it panted from the humidity.

The Samoyed and I locked eyes, and he ran over to me, breaking free of his owner. He jumped on me, two paws on my shoulders like I was being knighted or something, and I put my arms around his neck.

"He's a great hugger," the owner said, and offered me some weed when he saw that I was crying.

I shook my head.

He then offered me a handful of strawberry Tic-Tacs and I accepted, the sugar spreading slowly across my tongue.

He asked me where I'm from, and I thought of saying Williamsburg but I just said Canada.

He smiled at me. "I'm from Dominican Republic."

I think of all the resort town pictures I've seen, of people excited to tell you they're going South for their vacations, and I think of how little of the place they'll actually get to see.

The only person I could think of from the Dominican is Junot Diaz, and I started to mention it, to gush about how much I loved *This Is How You Lose Her*.

"You're a writer?" he asked, and I nodded slowly.

"One day, there'll be material in all of this, you'll see." He started to walk away.

One day, I thought, I hope I'll have forgotten how painful this loneliness is. A few weeks ago, I looked at my wedding pictures. My favourite was the one where he's shoving a slice of spongy, heavily iced cake in my face, and I'm laughing. The cake was tasteless but it was my only spontaneous smile. I thanked him and patted his Samoyed one more time as I found myself walking past the curled up, sleeping lizards back to my parents' apartment.

Rats in Disguise

I CAN STILL SEE MYSELF standing there, the small, reused brown box in my open palm. My mom had to remind me that it was Aunt Felicia's birthday. I think all she wanted me to do was write her a card, but I did one better. I went into my jewellery collection and pulled out some of my favourite pieces. I was into making necklaces, nothing too complicated. I used a piece of black leather cord, eighteen inches, and then I went through some of my favourite charms and beads. I found a pewter squirrel. It reminded me of one of my first days in Toronto, back when I'd only seen a squirrel at the zoo. Aunt Felicia's husband, Clive, stood behind me as I stared out of their kitchen window. "Wow, look at it flicking its tail," I said, and he wrinkled his nose. "It's just a rat in disguise, man," he said, his South African accent somehow heavier than mine, and walked away. I kept watching it, climbing and jumping around. I thought it was beautiful.

I moved the pewter squirrel to the middle of the cord. I thought about my Moroccan great grandmother, who believed so strongly in warding off the evil eye, she gave us all blue glass beads when we were born. I bought a bunch of similar ones, in turquoise and dark blue. I even bought more expensive blue stones like Sodalite and Lapis Lazuli, for good luck. I decided, since it was her birthday, I'd use one of each, on each side of the squirrel. I grabbed the box and even found a piece of white tissue paper in my mom's desk drawer. I didn't tell my mom.

When we got there, my mom gave my aunt a caramel-coloured cashmere sweater. Felicia smiled with no teeth, the lines on the sides of her mouth deepening. "Thank you," she said, and when she got up to go to her closet upstairs, to put everything away, I followed her. I handed her the box and she tore it open.

I could tell when she looked at me that I'd gotten it wrong and I instantly felt stupid.

"This is so nice," she said, "but you know I'll never wear it." She leaned in close and I could smell her baby powder deodorant. "I only wear real jewellery." I knew what she meant. The women in my family wore precious stones and real gold. I thought about how many times she'd told my grandmother that my mom was the materialistic one, she was the sporty one, the down to earth one who didn't care about these things.

She opened her underwear drawer. She put the box inside and closed it again. "I won't wear it, but I'll keep it in a special place, okay?"

She put it beside an undershirt of my sister's that she'd left behind on one of her visits before we moved her. Lila must have been three.

A few years later she gave it back to me. I didn't know what to do with it, so I stuffed it into the back of my desk drawer, where I forgot about it for years.

Aunt Felicia and Clive had twin boys, Jaron and Eitan, both born in Canada. Jaron was everything they ever wanted, tall, good looking, popular, attuned to everyone's moods and feelings. He could watch golf or play basketball with his dad and have heart to hearts with his mom. Eitan earned the nickname Satan because he never listened to any teacher or babysitter or authority figure. At best, his teachers said, he was 'hyper social,' and would talk to anyone. At worst, he refused to cooperate or do anything he didn't want to do, which was most schoolwork. He was the kind of kid who refilled vodka bottles in the freezer with water, then got caught when his dad found the bottle frozen. He mellowed out and became a vegan when he got older, and then people called him Seitan, even though he also went gluten free. Jaron became the corporate Bay street lawyer everyone wanted him to be, and Eitan became an artist, like me.

Most of the walls in Felicia's house were bare except for some muted Judaica paintings featuring the Western wall, a rabbi with a white candy floss beard, downcast eyes and a Chanukiah, and a small painting of St. Martin in their kitchen, full of green hills and swirling ocean and some candy-coloured houses. For her art was just decor, it could be uplifting and happy, or sombre and religious and that was it.

Clive had told me once that he'd been in a punk band when he was in high school, but he gave it up as soon as he got to university. It was as if they thought that making art was as inevitable and pointless as a toddler's tantrums—the fantasy part of being a kid that you abandoned for common sense and financial stability as you got older.

I was a cautionary tale for most of the boys' life. My grades were only average until the year I started purposely failing. I'll never forget the look on my parents' face when I got a seventeen percent in grade ten geography. When I stopped taking math altogether. When I somehow got into art school. At least they could tell people I was in university. I think they imagined me becoming an elementary school art teacher, or an illustrator of children's books about animals or plants.

They didn't picture me spraying graffiti murals under highways and in the tunnels train pass through. They didn't imagine me taking photos of the people under bridges, beautiful, interesting people turning tricks or shooting up or dropping rocks into blue glass pipes while they laughed and let go. They never imagined all this stuff I was doing would be worth money, that rich people would pay for my prints, that I'd have a whole book of my photos that they could buy in a bookstore.

I think they were a tiny bit proud, but they wouldn't admit it. A black and white photo book about people escaping their lives and doing too much Fentanyl is not exactly something to brag about, in their opinion. When the newspaper ran one of my photos, on the front page, to highlight the opioid epidemic, my dad told me he wanted to show everyone he knew, but the subject gave him pause.

My parents made me wash my hands when I walked in their front door. My mom offered to rewash my clothes, and they came out slightly shrunk and reeking of Tide.

When I really got into trouble, I didn't tell them. When I got raped I went to a Planned Parenthood alone, my hoodie pulled down so low you could only see my eyes. When I did drugs, and it got out of control, I told my parents I kept falling asleep because I had an eating disorder, and they sent me to outpatient treatment which actually did help.

I always shielded them from the worst things, and my parents' shame shielded me even more, so if Felicia says she knew about any of these things, she was lying.

When I was in high school Felicia got annoyed when my friends ran up to her, thinking she was my mom. Even when my friends were the good kids, I don't think she ever wanted to know anything about them or me or my life.

My mom wanted them to be closer than they were.

"I only have one sister," she kept telling anyone who would listen.

"But she doesn't like us," Lila and I would take turns saying in response, and eventually, she stopped trying so hard.

When we visited her back when I was nine, Felicia and I ran around making up songs, dancing and laughing. I hardly knew her, but I felt so comfortable. She kept telling me how much she loved me, how sad she was that she missed out on so much of my little kid life. I can only remember her coming home to visit us twice. Once, she took me swimming, and I tore open my hand trying to impress her by climbing the pool fence soaking wet. She said the gate was stuck, and she said she bet that I couldn't climb over the fence. I bet her I could. I got four stitches between my thumb and my first finger and Felicia didn't act like it was a big deal, so I didn't know it was until I saw my parents. The doctor said the stiches would dissolve on their own, but they didn't, so I pulled them out myself. I have a noticeable scar even today.

The other thing I remember about that day was my navy-blue full piece bathing suit. It was a speedo with a Criss Cross back, and I liked it. Felicia told me to look around, that she'd take me shopping for a bikini like some of the other girls were wearing. I looked down at my pooch of a stomach and shook my head. She looked back at me, her eyes glinting with another challenge.

The other time, she was at our house, after school, helping Lila and I with our homework. I was painting a scene from Pearl S. Buck's *The Good Earth* on the envelope I was handing my paper in. I used real rice from our pantry for the rice fields. Felicia wrinkled her nose when she saw the mess I was making.

She praised Lila for filling in her math sheets really quickly.

"I wish I could paint," Lila said.

"I mean, if anyone could choose between being good at math, or being good at the arts, they'd choose math, Lila. It's so practical."

When my parents said we were moving to Toronto, I was so happy. Felicia made me want to be braver even if I knew she didn't care about what happened to me.

It was different once we actually got here. When we temporarily moved in with them. When we heard Felicia and Clive fighting at night, Clive asking when we were going to leave.

Aunt Felicia was suddenly always working. When she wasn't working, she was working out, and when she wasn't working out, she was doing whatever Uncle Clive wanted.

"You know, sometimes divorce is a good thing," I remember my grandmother yelling at her one day.

Everyone hated Clive, because he was cold and indifferent to our family, because he was lazy and she out earned him, but most of all, because everyone knew he didn't love her. There were times when I sat on her car, listening to him yelling at her over her Bluetooth. At the end of the call, she'd always say "I love you," and he'd snap "me too" or say nothing at all.

I didn't see Aunt Felicia or Uncle Clive much after they had the twins. Clive started making more money and they moved into a McMansion. Their house was always chaotic. They had a full-time nanny, and a girl who lived a few houses down babysat so they could go on dates. They never wanted me to be around their kids, but occasionally Clive would want to take me to disturbing indie movie that Felicia would never want to see, or go see a band in a dive bar she'd never set foot in. It wasn't like having an uncle, or even a friend. It was like having hope that, one day, we'd all feel like family, like one day I'd meet people who wouldn't think I was a total weirdo.

Felicia always tried to teach me about men. "Even if you have a guy's kids, it's important that he always sees you as a woman." I nodded, even though I didn't know what she meant.

She was always doing squats while she talked, teaching me all her diet tricks including avoiding oils and dressings on salads, always drinking tons of water and pouring vinegar on her food so she wouldn't want to actually eat it.

When Clive inevitably left her for Ashley, his business partner's wife, who they'd double dated with and vacationed with multiple times, she started spending more time with my family. One night over dinner, I told her she was prettier that Ashley, and Lila pointed out how much Ashley looked like Steven Tyler. For a while, it seemed like our relationship would change, and it did, until she met the next guy. Then the guy after him.

Jaron became a huge success, and Eitan drifted all the way into a unit in my apartment building.

At first I was weary of him, having never been close growing up, but after a while it felt kind of nice to be so close to someone in my family.

He'd always loved tattoos. At first, when his parents asked, he blamed me for being a bad example and having them first, but now he admitted that he'd just told them what he knew they'd wanted to hear.

He had full sleeves, and designs on his back and legs. It didn't take long for him to apprentice at a tattoo parlour, and soon he had a huge clientele, even a few local celebrities.

He came over one night with his tattoo pen, needles and ink.

"I can't believe I haven't done you yet. What do you want?"

I had done a camera on my left wrist, and fluorescent beautiful graffiti that I designed myself across my shoulders. Then I thought about squirrels, their bushy tails, their curious eyes, always planning ahead for winter. I thought about the nests they slept in outside my window, the way they piled on top of each other, all breathing in unison. I thought about the daredevil types I saw in the dead of winter, heavier than normal, leaping off telephone wires and onto tree branches, but somehow, still making it.

I found the squirrel charm at the back of my drawer. "Give me one like this," I said, and pointed to the fleshy spot on the inside of my right arm. I told him the story about his dad and me, looking out the window. He showed me a sketch, where he added a tiny top hat and a diamond necklace. He drew one for himself, with a bowtie. When he was finished we'd officially match, two squirrels who had wandered far from the nest, but who'd somehow made it to a better place.

Together We Stand

I DON'T REMEMBER HOW WE MET. Everyone says it was in preschool, but I couldn't tell you what we said to each other, or what games we played, aside from the class's pile of ratty haired Barbies. There's a photo of us on Purim, you're resplendent in a peach satin dress, the perfect Queen Esther, and I'm wearing my grandmother's shiny gold trench coat with a tiara. There are seven other Queen Esther's in our class which infuriates me. I'm standing with my arms crossed.

"I'm going to be a fairy princess," you said, always the practical one. "You can be Queen Vashti."

I have another of us in my backyard. I'm wearing a big pink sweater, you're wearing a jean jacket that covers most of you and our expressions are very serious. Once we were friends we were friends with a capital F. We held hands. We were the silent person standing beside the other at all times.

You never forget your very first friend.

We'd go over to your house after school and watch Disney movies. We saw *Alice in Wonderland* at least five times. We ate thin strips of steak that had been smothered in barbeque sauce. At my house we ate homemade fries or barbequed corn.

"It was so much easier last year," you said. "When we were in kindergarten, we could come home earlier and sleep whenever we wanted."

I laughed because I thought you were being ridiculous.

In my house, you sucked it up until you weren't even sure what you were feeling. When I cried my parents reminded me that no one had died. I didn't know how to process my own feelings.

I was happy mostly, but there were huge stretches of time when I would zone out. I remember staring at the days of the week on the wall in grade one classroom, reflecting on it being Wednesday and the next moment, I was sitting at my desk and it was Friday.

It drove my mother crazy, that I had a place to escape to that she couldn't touch. Her yells would turn into background noise, and my head would turn off, first my thoughts and then my ears and then the rest of me.

Your favourite character was Eeyore from *Winnie the Pooh*. Mine was Ariel from the *Little Mermaid*. I drove you crazy constantly singing "Part of Your World."

"Don't you think Ursula is more interesting?" you asked.

That's the thing, you were always interesting.

You remember my birthday parties as being extravagant and over the top. You remember the guy with the cotton candy machine, the magician and his real white rabbits, the time my parents rented four ponies for two hours for all the kids in our class to ride on.

I remember your parties at your townhouse. I remember the way we sang *happy birthday*, the loot bags your mom made us, the way you complained, the way everything felt warm and like home.

It was just you and your mom, but you never acted like you were missing something. Your mom had a close friend who acted like an uncle, and he was kind to me too.

We both had moms who thought we were fat. My mom was always changing what I was eating, telling people I was a difficult eater. Our moms signed us up for ballet. Mine was mortified when I couldn't follow along, when I kept going to the bathroom instead of focusing and trying.

Your mom dragged us to aerobics classes. I remember bopping up and down beside her and you, we were maybe ten, and the song that played was "Itsy Bitsy Teeny Weeny Yellow Polka Dot Bikini."

We went for dinner with your mom after and filled up on breadsticks and Diet Coke.

There was the time I took an ice cream bar out of the freezer, chocolate covered, full of caramel and nuts and I smeared it on my homework. My parents were furious when they had to initial it before I could hand it in.

There was the time we went on vacation and my parents took me to my first diner. I ate my first ice cream sundae, complete with whipped cream and nuts, chocolate sauce and a cherry and I rhapsodized about it to my dad.

He grimaced. "It's not nice to talk about food that way," he said, so I stopped.

There was the time my dad dropped me at your house and chastised me for forgetting to brush my teeth before I left. "Get something to eat, when you get there, anything to hide the smell."

I asked for chocolate that day, Aeros and Smarties and when I swallowed them I didn't feel guilty.

There was a time when I got weighed after school. For a week, and then a month I had to cut out all sweets. I ate three Smarties that a friend gave me at school, green, pink and brown, and worried it would affect my weight. I remember the relief hitting the back of my knees so hard I almost had to sit.

There was the time that I searched the kitchen for sweets once I had reached her goal, first the pantry, then the fridge, and when I found nothing I searched the freezer. Half of my *My Little Pony* ice cream cake was still left from my birthday. I cut a piece. The neon pink part tasted gooey, but I swallowed, along with chunks of ice. An hour later I was vomiting out of control, on the kitchen tiles, in the hallway. My house had always been pristine, and my mother was so angry with me, for eating it, for being so out of control, every time I vomited I got a slap to the face, or the arm or the head.

I tried to tell her that I couldn't stop, I couldn't help it, but more vomit came out. There were other times, but it's the time I remember the most, the complete and total fear. I never told you.

I never even knew your dad's name, until you got really sick. You were sweating at night, you said. It was so ironic, you always wanted to lose weight, and now thirty pounds came off without even trying, but you knew it wasn't good.

Your dad was living across the world, and he wanted to come and see you, and I was incensed on your behalf, but I said nothing. You didn't let him, of course. You owe him nothing. This is the guy who abandoned you, I eventually told you, when you were small and adorable and perfect, when you first became my best friend. When your cousin confronted me at a party, I snapped at her that it was your choice, and she didn't know anything so she should stay out of it, and I don't know who was more surprised, me or her.

I surprised you when I told you I remembered your Hebrew name, when a rabbi came to our door asking for charity and I asked him to pray for you. It felt like you were standing right behind me, eight-year-old you, whispering it in my ear. Batya. Daughter of God. You were touched, you said you didn't remember mine, and I thought, I hope you never have to.

You were the kind of person who could complain about anything, how hard school was, how hard getting into college was, how hard work was, "it's the way it is." but when it came to fighting for your life no one fought like you. No one knew how to grit their teeth, how to tuck wavy tendrils behind their ears how to flash a smile that delights while it also says don't fuck with me. Anyone who says they can't believe you survived stage four cancer is an idiot. It was never about the odds, it was about you.

You're still the person I tell first when something bad happens, when someone rejects me, when something doesn't work out, when I had a miscarriage at almost twelve weeks pregnant, when I took the pills that made my body convulse and bleed, when I saw the grey sac that looked like a tiny baby with visible features plop into the toilet, I wanted to call you. I didn't want anyone else. I didn't want false reassurances, or toxic positivity. I wanted someone to tell me the truth, that life was terrible sometimes but we hold hands and we stand up slowly and hopefully we survive.

Born, Not Made

When I was a teenager, I didn't think I'd live to be twenty-one. I didn't know why, to be honest. It was just a premonition that felt true. I didn't get through things by imagining that one day I'd create some art from the experiences. I survived thinking one day I'll be able to buy a shovel big enough to bury all of this in someone's backyard, and I'll never have to think about it again.

I blocked a lot of details from my mind, so when I go back and try to recall them now, there are blanks, events and chunks of time that are missing. I wonder if I'll ever get them back. I wonder if I want to. Before we moved to Canada, my mom had told me that she was moving for my sister Taryn and I, for our futures, for our safety. She'd wanted to do it all along, we knew, but my dad wanted her to stay. Then my grandparents were in an armed robbery in their house. It was seven at night, still light outside, and they were eating dinner in their kitchen. No one was killed, but they were hit and kicked and shoved under the table. My mom says my skin as soft as my grandma's, we both bruise like peaches. They had to be quiet unless one of the guys was asking them where their valuables were. When we got there, hours later, the drawers were all emptied out, there were crushed lipsticks and feathers from duvets and pillows torn apart. There were clothes on the floor, plastic hangers snapped in half, a sun hat crushed by a heavy shoe. My eyes couldn't take in all the chaos, my grandparents were always so fastidious, obsessive even, about cleanliness.

It was my job, my mom told me, to be well adjusted. It was going to be harder for my mom than it was for us. She was a well liked and respected doctor. No one would know her in Canada. Taryn was little, and I was young enough, she reminded me. Kids were resilient, everyone knew that. But bouncing back when you don't know the social codes or rules, when you have nothing in common with people is basically impossible. I learned to fake it around my mom.

Once a week, on a Friday night, the three of us would have a long, involved, traditional Jewish Friday night dinner, with grape juice and challah bread, roasted chicken and potatoes and salad and chopped liver. It was the only night when things weren't rushed. My mom would ask me how my day was, and I'd say fine, and she'd move on to Taryn, who was more expansive. Taryn instantly made friends. Taryn's teachers thought she was adorable. If my mom asked who my friends were, I'd tell her about my favourite characters in the books I was reading. She believed me, but then my memory for details was excellent, and her interest in me was always superficial.

On the weekends, my sister would get together with friends. Taryn had always been sweet and funny but back home she nearly constantly threw tantrums, bashing her baby teeth up into her gums when we played hide and seek, going headfirst into a wall at one of my birthday parties. She was the world's pickiest eater, something my mom used to complain about endlessly, but now, she thought I was the difficult one.

There was a girl, Yvonne, a year older than me, who'd immigrated from Johannesburg at the same time. We'd gone to different schools, but we kind of knew each other. She was one of those obsessively normal people, someone who could pick up the trends and expressions and blend in, the kind of girl no one would ever be able to pick out of a line up. I was so jealous of her.

Yvonne walked with confidence. She lost her accent faster than me. I had to work at it. I watched a lot of bad American sitcoms about families who loved each other and kids who had the time of their lives in high school, cheerleaders and jocks and class presidents. I repeated phrases over and over so they sounded natural. "Yeah, right. I hate her guts. Oh My God."

I wasn't a bad student, but unlike at home, I wasn't an exceptionally good one.

Everything was different. Math was harder. The books we read were less interesting. I'd read under my desk when the teacher wasn't looking. Only one kid noticed.

"Any good?" he'd ask me, and sometimes we'd talk about books.

I wasn't used to being friends with boys. I found it hard to talk to him, though I always wanted to.

There was a boy named Erez who only ever talked to me in a slow, loud over-the-top South African accent that sounded slightly Texan. Our assigned lockers were beside each other, so there was no escaping him. He had curly hair, a wide forehead and wide gaped teeth that his braces couldn't fix. He was obsessed with all the popular girls, making up songs that he would sing them, buying them expensive chocolate for Valentine's Day.

There were seven of them, including Ruthie, a girl whose sister Annie was already good friends with my sister. She came up to me one day and told me that my mom asked her to look out for me. A few weeks later we went to the mall together, ate French fries and even took those cheesy photo booth pictures. I thought I'd finally made a friend. The next day, I put the photos up in my locker, like I saw everyone else do.

Erez grabbed the photo, tore it up and threw it into the industrial sized garbage at the end of the hallway.

"Ruthie's my friend," I protested and Erez snorted. "No she isn't."

Later that day, in class I was so sure that she'd be upset with him, that when he told me, like he always did that I was a loser with no friends, I looked in her direction, and said: "Ruthie's my friend."

Erez looked at her and laughed like it was the best joke he'd ever heard. "Ruthie, you want me to tell her? Are you really friends with *her*?"

Ruthie fixed me with the same big smile she'd had on the first time we'd talked.

"Of course," she said, in an over-the-top cheery voice, "I'm everybody's friend."

Another boy, Judah, had a long, thin nose, beady eyes, and sharp looking canines. He scuttled like a rat in the hallways. Together, he and Erez made fun of me while everyone either ignored them or laughed along.

One day, our French teacher was absent and a substitute did the attendance.

Instead of Lindi, she read my name as Linder. Linder Bumbum, instead of Lindy Buxbaum.

Judah thought this was hilarious. He lead the whole class in a chant.

"Buh buh buh buh buh buh, BUM," to the tune of Charge! Like at a baseball game.

The class would chant it, then look at me, and I would slide down in my chair, trying to disappear.

The teachers would look away, like they couldn't hear anything. I'd never thought about my ass being big before but I started asking my mom to buy me bigger clothes, and tying sweatshirts around my waist.

Judah would make kids playlists, individualized and thoughtful, which slowly made him more popular.

"Bum, I made you one," he said one day, and I was stupid enough to ask to hear it.

It had one song on it, which I'd never heard of, called "Mr. Personality." I think it was from the 1990's.

Over the chorus, Judah sang his own version: "They call her Lindi personality because she's so ugly!"

Nathan stood behind him, laughing so hard he had to wipe his eyes.

The worst thing happened at Zev Epstein's bar mitzvah. Even if you had no friends, you got invited, because everyone invited the whole class.

Every table had centrepieces made of silver balloons and a heavy weight.

I ate chicken for dinner. I danced to ancient dance music, including the YMCA, and the Macarena.

In the passage that led into the party room were stacks of extra chairs, five or six heavy piles of metal, padded chairs. Everyone was inside unless they had to leave to go the bathroom.

Erez and Judah were waiting for me in between the chairs. One of them was holding extra centrepieces, the other one held me so I couldn't move.

I didn't scream, but even if I had, the music was so loud, no one would have heard me. I'm not sure they would have cared if I had.

They used five centrepieces in all, tied my hands and feet, and the back of my hair to a stack. If I moved, I threatened to bring a whole stack of chairs down on me. I was around five feet tall, and each stack was over six feet at least.

Nobody freed me. Eventually my mom came to pick me up. I watched the colour drain out of her face when she saw me, trapped there. She used her car keys to cut the ribbons.

The school's principal said, "It happened on a weekend, not on school property, so there's nothing we can do."

My mom didn't offer to let me move schools, so I didn't ask.

She channelled her rage into changing my behaviour. "What did you do," she asked, "to make them make fun of you?" And then, trying to be practical: "Let's make a list of all the things you can change and do to make kids like you."

I stopped talking for a long time. If I didn't say anything, no one could make fun of me.

When I got home, it was weird to have to start talking again, so sometimes I didn't. I chewed a lot of gum. I went online a lot. I talked into my sleeves.

"Teenagers mumble," my mom told anyone who asked. "It's totally developmentally appropriate."

I read a lot. I drew sometimes. I listened to music.

I spent my lunches either in the bathroom or in the school library. I read just about everything in their fiction section, from *The Hobbit* to Holocaust literature.

I got skinnier. I tried my hardest to disappear.

They say artists are born, not made. It's true that I was always a weirdo. It's true that drawing and writing were my favourite things to do as a kid. I like creating imaginary worlds. I had imaginary friends way longer than it was normal to. It's also true that, if none of these things had happened, they might have remained hobbies. When I lived to be twenty-one, I officially decided to make the most of my life. If I hadn't needed to become invisible for so long, I might never have needed any recognition.

Would You Rather?

WE WERE HAVING STICKY, cheese oozing pizza with a family who were friends with my mom. We sat at two tables under the red awning of an Italian restaurant patio, the adults at one, us kids at another. We were supposed to use a knife to cut it, but when the adults turned their backs preoccupied, we tore into it with our hands. Just to our left, jacaranda trees dropped their soft, lilac petals and leaves. The air smelled musky, like honey and earth mixed with bubbling mozzarella and grease. My sister Taryn pretended to gag before we even sat down. She fluttered her thick, dark eyelashes and made a throaty hiss, and my mom reassured her that she'd feel better once she ate something. I rolled my eyes. My mom's friend Eleanor had gone to medical school with her, and her husband sold scrubs and medical supplies. I never knew what adults expected me to say when they shared that kind of information. Did they want me to act impressed? Did they hope I'd tell them about school?

My mom insisted that we'd met them before, but neither of us could remember. Samantha was a year older than me, and the son, Brett, was about Taryn's age. They started talking right away, while Samantha and I picked at the basket of bread sticks in front of us. Samantha had chest length, wavy blond hair, exactly like Taryn's Skipper doll, and she was wearing gold, sparkly eye shadow. My mom never let us wear makeup. When I told her I liked it, she shrugged and said her aunt let her buy or use whatever she wanted.

"I have a cool aunt too," I said. "But she lives in Canada."

"You probably just think she's cool because you don't actually live with her."

I blinked at her. "What?"

"Eleanor's not my mom, Lindi, she's my aunt."

"Oh. So how come you live with her?"

"My parents and my real brother were killed two years ago in a carjacking. I wasn't there because I was at a dance class. But I almost missed it. I was almost there …"

"So Brett …"

"Is my cousin. My mom and Eleanor were sisters."

"That's terrible," I said, feeling like an idiot, not knowing what else to say.

"What's terrible," she said, "is how hard everyone tries to be nice to me. I get the feeling she'd get me anything I wanted …"

I almost laughed. That didn't sound bad at all.

"Who, Eleanor?"

"*Ja*, and like, everyone. Teachers, friends' moms, friends. Sometimes I want to just say to them, life is awful, and you can't give me what I want anyway, so fuck off and stop trying."

Samantha looked over at Eleanor, her cheeks turning slightly pinker. She spoke even more quietly. "But I can't, because Eleanor and Mark invited me to live with them, and I have to be grateful."

She smiled a perfect, white picket fence smile.

"It's what my mom would have wanted."

Later we talked about where both of our families were moving to. They were going to Australia, eventually. I told her that my dad and his new wife had just moved there.

"To Sydney? That's where we're supposed to be going."

I shook my head. "Melbourne. They started a new dental practice there."

I told her the story, the one I never tell anyone, about my dad leaving us for his younger receptionist/hygienist, like the plot in one of those TV shows my mom never wants me to watch.

Taryn overheard and looked at me with raised eyebrows.

I shrugged back.

"Would you rather have a dad that dies when you're a young, or a dad who leaves, moves halfway across the world, and never calls you?"

Samantha took a sip of her Diet Coke.

She shrugged. "I don't know. At least if he's alive, there's still a chance."

I thought about Kate, my new stepmother, and how she was sixteen weeks pregnant now with twins. When my dad had new kids, I knew, any chance of him ever visiting was over.

"Don't worry," she said, looking straight at me, a half-smile on her lips. "I'm sure your mom will remarry too."

I actually laughed. "Not likely," I said. "She doesn't even want to."

* * *

Even after three years, I wasn't great at making friends in Toronto. I was managing at school, and my mom didn't seem to mind that I spent a lot of my free time reading. Every weekend Taryn had plans, playdates and get togethers and parties, and I didn't. My mom tried to make me feel better by including me in her plans. We explored Toronto together, from Greektown to Chinatown to Little India. We tried a lot of new foods, but we didn't talk much.

Sam and I kept in touch. First the family moved to Sydney, and then after two years they moved to West Bloomfield, a suburb near Detroit with a big Jewish community.

"Would you rather be a weirdo with no friends in one city, or two cities?" she emailed me.

My dad's one gift to me over the last five years was a laptop which was as heavy as his old toolbox.

"Would you rather have a chance to start over, or be stuck in the same place?" I answered.

"Would you rather have your house broken into, and lose everything you're sentimental about, or keep everything, move to a new country and get bullied?" she wrote me late one night.

"Would you rather keep all your stuff, but lose any sense of who you are, and why that should matter?" I wrote back but then deleted it before I sent it. I wasn't sure she'd understand.

* * *

Sam was right, my mom did remarry and at least on paper, things were better. We lived in a bigger house, and my mom worked less. My stepdad, Barry, was an ophthalmologist, and he seemed to hardly work, but he made more money than my mom. He had a private clinic where he did laser eye surgery, and a couple of days a week he worked in the same hospital as my mom, treating patients with glaucoma or cataracts. They got married at a resort in Jamaica, after dating for less than a year. He was tall and skinny, with salt and pepper hair and skin that turned tomato red at the first sign of sun. At first, Taryn called him the Pink Panther. Like everyone else, he liked her better than me. He said he found her "easier to relate to". One night I heard him tell my mom he wanted to legally adopt her, and then I heard my mom say, "What about Lindi?" And then I couldn't hear the rest. It only got worse after our mom had her third kid, our baby sister, Rina. Taryn was the built-in babysitter of their dreams, and I couldn't get out of the house fast enough.

Sam's aunt let her come visit us over December break. My mom bought a second twin bed to put in my room. We pushed our beds together so we could talk late at night. We weren't allowed to do much, besides go see movies, and the mall. One day we walked down the street and followed a neon sign to a tattoo parlour that was set up in someone's basement. We got tiny purple flowers on our ankles, like the jacarandas that fell around us that first day we met. We covered them with our socks. We used witchhazel we found in my mom's closet to keep them clean.

Another day we got the cartilage in our right ears pierced at Claire's. Later that night Sam told me to switch earrings so "we'd be real blood sisters."

We ended up giving each other infections and having to take them out.

"Would you rather have a blood sister you're close to, or a real sister that you're not?" she asked me.

I said I wished she was my real sister, and then I could have both.

She smiled.

"Would you rather have a close blood sister, or your real brother back?"

She didn't answer me, then she turned off the light.

Later that week we went to a cheesy horror movie, and Sam ordered nachos with cheese, popcorn with extra butter, Kit Kats, Twizzlers. She took the tiniest bites of everything.

"The trick," she said with authority, "is to taste everything, without actually eating much."

I rolled my eyes. "I swear, if you say 'nothing tastes as good as being thin' I'll hit you over the head with this pack of Twizzlers."

She laughed. "I know, I probably sound like those stupid girls at your school, but it is true."

"Would you rather be fat, and accepted and loved by everyone at your school, or skinny and beautiful, and kind of lonely?" I asked her.

"Skinny and beautiful, obviously." She laughed and slapped my knee.

"Would you rather be skinny and beautiful, or really smart?"

I shook my head. I wanted to tell her that they both felt like a fantasy to me, but she looked at me with big expectant eyes, and I knew what I was supposed to say.

"I'd rather be smart," I said quietly, and she smiled, seemingly satisfied.

After the movie, she told me about how, as a little kid, relatives and friends would tell her that she was beautiful, and she'd laugh and fluff out her curls, look them right in the eye and say, "I know." It was one of the only times she could remember her mother ever getting angry with her. "Don't be so arrogant," she'd say, and Sam would look at her with her big green eyes and say she was sorry.

"I was being sarcastic," she said, and she laughed. "I didn't really mean it. Who really thinks they're beautiful?"

"I know," I said. "I get it."

When Sam recommended a six-week sleepover camp in the Adirondacks, I mentioned it to my mom and she signed me up right away. Her aunt pulled some strings so that even though she was a year older we were put in the same cabin. The American kids were friendlier, and there were a handful of kids from my school in Toronto, who acted like they were meeting me for the first time. At least they were nicer now. Two of them asked to borrow my clothes, and one of them even hugged me sometimes. I tried to pretend that all of it was normal.

We did all the things I expected we'd do: we slept in bunk beds, Sam insisted on the top bunk so I was below. We walked around the field to the dining hall wearing our new white skin-tight T-shirts. Hers said Hottie in bright purple letters, and mine said Fresh in hot pink. When we heard two girls in our cabin talking about us Sam just said it meant we were doing things right. When a younger girl made fun of my moss green toenails, Sam told her to fuck off. We went swimming, canoeing and sailing. We even went on a small camping trip. We slept in the same tent as two other girls, Marnie and Jamie. Late one night I heard Sam and Marnie, talking outside the tent, by the small fire our councillors had built.

"So, Lindi's like, your best friend?"

"She's a friend I knew from back in South Africa, but she can be very clingy. I need space to have new experiences, and I don't know how to tell her."

I stumbled back to the tent, wiped my eyes on the back of my hand, and pretended to be asleep.

There were only three weeks left of camp anyway. My mom and Barry and my sisters were in the Caribbean, because Barry had a timeshare, so it's not like I could have called them to come and pick me up. This was what normal kids did, so I decided to try to fit in.

"Would you rather lose your best friend, or lose who you used to be?" I asked her in my mind.

"Ha, trick question," I answered her, before she could say anything. "I lost both."

I traded clothes with other girls. I sat with them and listened to music and said I liked the same boys as them, and said I agreed about whoever they said was hot. A girl fell asleep next to the hotpot that was making her instant Mac and Cheese and got third degree burns all over her face that took all summer to heal. Another girl got kicked out for offering guys blowjobs in exchange for all of their smores.

Sam got involved with a popular guy in the oldest cabin. His name was Joey and, on one of the last nights of camp, she slept with him. She didn't tell me, but everyone in our cabin knew so that's how I found out. I didn't even kiss anyone.

"People drift," my mom said, shrugging when I mentioned it to her that fall.

"Obviously," I said, and I didn't know how to explain that a lot of the time I was scared that I was too much for people, and until I heard her say it, I thought that Sam understood me.

I looked at my mom, hoping she would reassure me that eventually I'd find people who loved me for who I was, but she just patted my shoulder and said she had to get dinner ready before Barry and Taryn got home. I wished I belonged with them as seamlessly as they fit with each other. I went upstairs, wondering if I'd ever meet the people who would feel like my real family.

His Forever Girl

"I COULD SEE US doing this forever, Lindi," Brandon said one day.

"Really?" I tried to hide the hope that came rushing into my voice.

"Sure. I could see us getting married—to different people, you to some guy, me to some girl, but us keeping this up, you and me, for always."

I swallowed hard. I wasn't sure what to say and he didn't seem to notice.

* * *

The summer after grade nine was a game changer. I grew my hair long and hung out with my older cousin Casey, who introduced me to her cool friends. Nothing happened, but guys hit on me for the first time. It was embarrassing to be fifteen and have never kissed anyone.

I had another friend who was in the same boat as me, but she was a really good student, top three percentile of our grade, so she had an excuse. I was too average to pretend that I had the kind of focus that superseded boys.

I was too old for school agenda books so I bought a small, thick blue notebook with two Sailor Moon stickers, that I got for a dollar from a gumball machine in the supermarket. He was sitting right in front of me, slight with short, floppy brown hair and piercing blue eyes. He looked like a troubled Timothee Chalamet.

He turned around, grabbed the notebook off my desk and started flipping through it. There was nothing in it, really, just homework assignments. He smiled at the stickers on the cover, kept the book and turned around to face the teacher.

I tried to ignore him even as I felt my cheeks getting hot. He took a white graffiti marker. A few minutes later, he handed it back to me. Both stickers were covered, and on top of one of them he'd written Sailor Penis.

I rolled my eyes and flipped open the first page. On my list it now said, don't forget to text Brandon, along with his phone number. I tapped his shoulder.

"You have to fix this," I said, pointing to the sticker. He crossed out the word Penis and scribbled in Beautiful. He turned back around before I could react.

It took me a week to text him. We went back and forth for two hours, a lot of GIFs, and memes and stupid stuff, music he liked, cars, which I didn't care about but we were talking, and that made everything matter less.

Livia lived on the next street, and we were in the same grade. I hated her, but we got thrown together a lot, so everyone thought we were friends, including her. She had a head like a pumpkin and when she got excited and smiled she looked like a jack-o-lantern. She had a small pot belly but swore she had great abs. Her mom was a tailor and their upstairs hallway was full of creepy, half-dressed mannequins. Her dad was on a macrobiotic diet, and was always eating disgusting bowls of amaranth and tofu next to steaming piles of dandelion. She'd hooked up with, and almost went all the way with, a guy she met on a family yoga retreat in Maui. She laughed when I told her I had a crush on Brandon.

"You know you have no chance with him, right?"

A few days later, we hung out in the gazebo across the street from school. He rolled his own cigarettes and we shared one.

"Do ever think about how it would be to have a friend to experiment with? So there's no pressure, and everything can just be fun?"

I wasn't sure. "Yeah, maybe," I murmured and he dropped it.

I heard Livia's voice over and over in my head. We started walking and before we got to the subway, I found myself saying: "Having a person to experiment with could be good." After that he acted like it was all my idea.

He even told our mutual friend, Talia, who pressed me for details. After I went over to his house for the first time, he told her that nothing had actually happened.

"Don't you think Talia would be hot if she lost weight?" he asked me. She had a great, white smile, naturally tan skin and springy dark curls. She had wide hips, and full thighs. I thought she looked like one of those classic movie stars, but she'd wave her hands dismissively whenever I said it. She was always trying to lose weight.

She stared at me when I ate fries.

"You're so lucky you don't have to diet," she said.

"Of course I have to diet, everyone has to," I said. I thought about how often I walked or ran, or drank diet coke, and when really desperate, threw up.

"I was looking at you the other day in French. I was thinking, wow, you really are skinny."

"Was I wearing my purple shirt?"

She nodded.

"It was definitely the shirt," I said. "It's too big, I bought the wrong size."

She rolled her eyes. "I bet Brandon liked it. Easy access."

Talia was the only person who knew. She told me what he'd told her, and I told her the truth but made her promise never to tell. I knew they studied together sometimes too, but he usually didn't talk about her.

"I think she's pretty the way she is," I said to him, and he shook his head.

"I just think she'd look better if she looked more like you," he answered, and I knew it was supposed to be a compliment but it made me feel sick.

* * *

That first time, we were lying on the beige carpeted floor of his bedroom. Everything was beige: his desk, his bed linen, the walls. There were posters of red, shiny BMW's and silver Aston Martin's above his bed.

He reached for my hand to pull me up and held it and didn't let go. It felt electric.

"So," he said, smiling at me, "are you going to start, or should I?"

"What? I …"

He kissed me. I tried to use my tongue—wasn't that what you were supposed to do?—but he shook his head.

"It's gross."

"Okay," I said, and he kissed me again. He slipped a hand under my shirt.

I was wearing jeans and a long-sleeved grey shirt with lace around the collar. I also wore a lace bra. I wanted to look nice, but not like I was trying too hard.

We didn't go that far the first time. I didn't take my shirt off. On my way out, he told me he wanted to be my boyfriend, but he didn't want anyone to know.

I reached over and kissed him on his porch, with my dad waiting in the car. Brandon looked startled but kissed me back.

His two best friends didn't like me. "They always make fun of you," he'd told me in the gazebo one day. I knew I shouldn't, but I asked why.

"The way you dress," he said. "All the bright colours. All the attention you're probably seeking."

"I just like the colour orange."

"And the way you are in class, you know, when you don't make eye contact with teachers."

"I'm shy."

"I know that. But they think it's weird."

The biggest thing, really, was that I wasn't popular enough. His ex-girlfriend, Kelsey, was short, with blonde hair that she flat ironed straight, thick bangs, and big green saucer eyes. She wasn't beautiful, but she treated looking cute like a critical life skill. All her friends dressed alike, expensive but well-worn jeans, T-shirts you had to be rich to afford. I only knew her because the year before, my friend Shelly, who didn't go to our high school, but knew Kelsey and her crew from camp, invited them and me over for a sleepover. Once she changed the location to my house, Kelsey and every single one of her friends gave me a lame excuse for why they couldn't be there. We'd ignored each other ever since.

Brandon came up to me in the hallway, looking around to make sure we were alone.

"Look, I know I said we could be boyfriend and girlfriend, but I don't think we should. Let's just go back to being friends."

"What? Why?"

"The way you kissed me before you left, anyone could have seen you."

I stared at him. "No one saw."

"But they could have. I can only do this with someone discreet."

He gave me a tight smile.

"I gotta go. Don't worry, we can still be friends."

He walked away, and I slid down, my backpack suddenly weighing me down.

He started texting me a lot again after that.

When we got together, we still fooled around. Sometimes he came over to my house, sometimes I went to his. I just wanted small things. To hold his hand in public, or for him to put his arm around me. To be able to tell him that I loved him, or to have him tell me. I was a good student, but when he asked me to skip class to hangout with him, I did it. All the private places were his idea. Behind the pizza store. In a hidden corner of the library. In the basement of a synagogue across the street. There was no illusion anymore about being boyfriend and girlfriend, but I couldn't stop hoping. I hated myself.

One day, he got a legitimate girlfriend. She didn't go to our school, but he'd show everyone photos of her, and his Instagram was full of her and him. Her name was Sadie and she was a friend of a friend, which made it much worse. I was fuming but I ignored him. He texted less, and then more again. As a kind of consolation, he invited me over. The first time I went down on him was when he was dating her. He invited me over on a Sunday, asked me to go down on my knees, and pushed my head back and forth. I almost threw up, but I guess those bouts of bulimia were good for something, because I stopped myself. When he was about to come, he helped me up, gently and said he'd finish in his garbage can. "I don't want you to have to know the difference between spitting and swallowing," he said, a tiny bit of tenderness in his voice. He refused, as always to reciprocate. He broke up with her the next day, which seemed like a sign but nothing changed between us. Occasionally I'd meet guys who'd ask me out, and he'd make fun of them relentlessly, telling me they weren't good enough for me.

I still helped him with his English homework. I wrote a poem that he handed in once, comparing falling in love to dropping acid, even though I hadn't ever. We'd just read *On the Road* and our teacher loved it. One night I stayed up all night helping him to write a paper. I didn't feel used as much as I felt useful, which was addictive. It made me feel smart, and when he gushed his gratitude after, calling me a princess and telling me I deserved every gesture in the world, it felt like it meant something.

Nothing changed until Talia confessed that she'd been spending time with Brandon too.

They'd stopped now, she swore, but she and Brandon had fooled around a few times. She'd been telling me for months about a guy she worked at the movie theatre with. It wasn't official either, so we both shared tons of graphic details.

She was unbelievably sorry. She really wanted to make it up to me. I walked away.

Brandon still texted me all the time, and I found it reassuring even if I didn't answer him.

There were times I'd still try to get his attention. I'd wear a maroon tie dye tank top he'd told me he liked, pull it down a little in front, and he'd look at me with pity, like it was sad that I was trying so hard.

After a few weeks, Talia told me she'd felt guilty for long enough and she couldn't go on apologizing and feeling bad indefinitely. She needed to move on, she said and cut me out of her life.

We finally hung out again in the gazebo. "I'm not your boyfriend," he said matter-of-factly.

I quoted him a line from one of his favourite British bands, something about feeling instantly replaced.

"I'm not your guy," he said, and there was no emotion in his voice, not even irritation. "I don't owe you anything."

We didn't talk for a long time after that. I dated a friend of his, and I finally publicly had a boyfriend. The spark didn't run so deep, but it was nice to know that it was possible. I told him about what had happened. "At least you'll be able to spot a liar now," he said, and I nodded, but it was more than that.

We lost touch for almost ten years. We were both single when he found me on a dating app. I didn't recognize him. He had a beard, his cheeks were fuller and his hair was short. His description read: Just Another Jewish lawyer. He sent me a message. He said he'd gone to law school in New Mexico and was living in Santa Fe. He was a criminal lawyer. I googled him for the first time in years. There was an article about a case he'd won, for a basketball coach who was accused of sexual assault. The phrase beyond a reasonable doubt appeared five times. The girl was seventeen.

He asked for my number, and he called me.

"I can't believe you didn't recognize me," he said.

"It's been a long time," I answered. "It's cool that you recognized me."

"Of course I did. How could I forget you?"

I laughed. I thought about the whole situation.

"I guess this makes me one of your favourite ex-girlfriends."

He paused. "You were never my girlfriend."

I took a deep breath. There was so much I wanted to say but I hung up instead. I'd looked at his social media earlier. His photos were a few years old and slightly more flattering. There was no sign of a girlfriend or a wife.

He was still friends with Talia who was married with three kids. She was skinny now, and she sold diet and work-out plans for a living.

I wondered if he made her feel like she was good enough now, if she was his forever girl, the one he kept see-ing even though they were both with other people.

The thought didn't bother me as much as it used to.

The Name Game

"I don't know where they are."
—Cat Power, Names

THEY CALLED HER PITS because her last name was Pitfield. Kids would sing "hands up baby hands up" and laugh whenever she raised her hand in class and they saw the jungle of brown hair, all dense and tangled like ferns growing wild. We were only twelve but the popular girls told everyone that she should have started shaving. One of their guys came up to her in the hall, heavy and imposing like a bouncer outside an adult event and asked her if her pits matched her carpet and she kicked him in the stomach with her steel toe boots. She told us in her low, measured baritone that it was totally worth getting suspended over.

They called her Dime Bag because she started a business making beaded necklaces, pastel daisy chains, with tiny little white flowers. She would sell them in the washroom at recess. I bought a lavender and baby pink choker that held together for ages. She was doing well until the most popular girl in our grade saw the little plastic bags and told everyone that she caught her dealing drugs (and later, that she found her decorating her own locker for her birthday, and no one could decide which was worse).

They called her Bisexual because, one day in science class when we were fourteen, the teacher asked us about the two types of reproduction. She looked up, a big grin across her still full, light acne pocked baby cheeks and said: "A sexual and Bisexual." Her face got hot and turned red, and she yelled something about not being one of those indecisive people who didn't know what they wanted, she liked men, just men for fuck's sake—and I wanted to throw my binder at her, because I was bi and I already knew it then, even if I hadn't told anyone yet.

They called her the Librarian because of a rumour that she'd had oral sex with a guy in our school library, in this hidden section off to the side, where people went to study. She read a lot, and you could find her scribbling furiously in her notebook. You could tell she was obsessed with him. She'd stare daggers when he flirted with other girls, but it never stopped him. A girl and her friend said they saw them, and the story changed from seeing them make out to hearing her tell her friend she went down on him there. His gay best friend, who was obviously in love with him, insisted they'd had gone all the way, had anal even, but when people asked her, and all she would say was that she was still a virgin.

They called her the Mattress when she was there to substitute for our favourite history teacher when I was fifteen. She was blonde, prettier than most teachers, with a slightly hooked nose that made her look interesting, too. She wore caramel V-neck sweaters, with the sleeves rolled up, and her hair pulled back, like she was ready to do serious work, which was bad news for the people in my class. One of them swore that her mom knew her back in the day, and that everyone called her the mattress because she made the rounds. She had a straight talking, comforting energy, and when I thought about Mr. A, who looked down the shirts of girls his daughter's age as he walked around the class, in exchange for easy A's, I felt sick.

They called her the Ditz because she could do a pitch perfect imitation of all those actresses in 90's classics, Cher from *Clueless*, Elle from *Legally Blonde*. She had the highest GPA in our grade, but it didn't matter. All everyone ever said was that she didn't have much substance, and I wish that I'd corrected them, even once, because I knew her better when I was fifteen.

They called her Miss Fist, even though she was the epitome of tiny and delicate, all polo shirts and blonde curly hair. She looked a lot younger than sixteen. Her boyfriend was a giant, but people insisted they saw them go under the bleachers at a school basketball game. She was a model of discretion, never saying a word to anyone, but whenever I saw his giant hands swallowing hers when I saw them walking around together, I tried not to flinch and wonder how much it hurt.

They called her Dee, which she insisted on, because her full name was Dikla, which meant palm tree in Hebrew, but when she used it, people started calling her dick lover. If someone forgot her name, she'd say Dee, like my bra size. She poured herself into too tight T-shirts and told everyone how she woke up one day and all of her bras and shirts were too small. I was sixteen, too old for things to change too much in that department, but her story made me hope it might. She wanted everyone to know that her boyfriend was her first, that she planned to marry him. It was important that they were each other's one and only, she told me, because it was the only way things could be meaningful. I'm ashamed of how much I hoped he'd cheat on her.

They called her The Crow because she painted her face like the guy in the movie, all powder white with thick black streaks and smeared lips, and she wore Pantera and Pop Will Eat Itself T-shirts. She and one of her boyfriends used to steal the scales from the Science Lab to weigh and sell their drugs. She didn't even consider me cool enough to tell me what they were selling.

"I weigh ninety-six pounds," she told me one day in gym class. "I'm worried about myself." And I was too jealous to say anything helpful.

They called her Janice, because she was 5"10, and rail thin, with dark hair, a new nose like Janice Dickinson, and a laugh as distinctive and honking as Janice on *Friends*. She'd get her hair blown out and her make-up done just to walk in our school's fashion show. She wore designer clothes with ironic jewellery, huge dollar store smiley face or large fake diamond rings. Her locker was full of weeks' worth of gourmet lunches that she'd never touched. I didn't know anyone could envy me until I saw her eyeing me after trying to flirt with the guy I was dating.

They called him JD, because he had James Dean hair, all pompadour-y soft and sticky with pomade. He could flirt with his eyebrows. He always smelled like CK One, mint gum and hand sanitizer that he used to hide the smell of his cigarettes. He could compliment you on the tiniest thing, your new jeans, the fact that you were wearing eyeliner, the band button on your jacket, and you'd feel like you were seen. He was always cutting class, smoking weed and drinking JD, like he knew how stupid everything we worried about was. He was intense about his acting. He said he wanted to direct, or act in something great. I wanted him to get to live in a world where it was safe to show a fuller range of emotions. He was murdered, in a case related to drugs and, when they invited me to a tribute night about his life, I couldn't bring myself to leave the house.

They called her Signs, because she had two deaf parents, and was fluent in sign language. She was always part of our school's play, signing beside an actor to the songs in *Cats* or *Mary Poppins*, like a bit of actual magic. She had a sweet, helium voice, and I thought if she could get a job as a cartoon or voiceover actor, she'd get rich. One day, she stopped wearing any tight shirts, including her favourite dark purple one, because her dad told her she looked like a whore. I wondered what the sign looked like, if his face got angry and red, if it made her cry.

A guy we knew saw her after she dropped out of school. He said, "Remember Signs? She's working as a cashier at The Shoe Company now. You know how she wasn't fat before, but she wasn't skinny? She's really skinny now."

I hope they're happier now.

I hope they've gotten kinder. I hope I have.

Aloha State

THEY SAT STIFFLY in their seats in the front row. Matt had paid an additional hundred dollars for the extra leg room and the only slightly wider armrests that invariably worked better for his wife than they did for him. He shifted his arm in irritation and looked behind him. They weren't quite in first class, a faded grey plastic wall and two fitting room-sized washrooms separated them, but they were slightly better off than the people sitting behind them in economy. Marcella had gripped his hand during the take off. She'd had her nails painted purple, and with each tiny ascension she'd dug them into the fleshy part of his hand, leaving tiny red half moons. He'd tried not to wince. He wasn't sure how to talk to her anymore.

The flight attendants came around with drink carts and a choice of a tiny bag of salty pretzels or dry, flavourless cookies. Marcella shook her head, but Matt took one of each. He ordered a glass of water, and she nodded, opened her mouth to ask for something too, but he interrupted her and ordered ginger ale.

"Lots of ice," he said.

"I have to go to the bathroom," she said, and he nodded.

It had only been a month, he reminded himself. He'd almost forgotten about the trip until he got an email reminder the week before.

They'd sat side by side on their cracked leather couch, a remnant from her childhood home that she couldn't bring herself to get rid of. She was emotional watching a contestant from *The Voice* get voted into the top ten. Haley was twenty-seven. She'd wanted to sing since she was a teenager, but her religious family had disowned her for being gay, and she'd only started again recently. Her wife cheered her on from the audience.

Marcella dabbed her eyes. "There's something so great about seeing people's dreams come true," she said quietly.

He pulled up his phone. "Do you still want to go to Honolulu?" he asked.

She breathed in loudly and nodded. "Yeah," she said, "I've always wanted to go."

* * *

Marcella stood in front of the airplane bathroom, rocking on the balls of her feet. She was wearing a pair of black beaten up flats that she had considered throwing away. She had mentioned it to Matt, but he'd shrugged. "It's a ten-hour flight, babe, wear whatever's most comfortable."

There were two people ahead of her in the line, an older woman, and a mom holding hands with a small, three-year-old girl. "I have to goooo," the kid said, whining. Marcella's nipples burned. She felt a strange mix of tenderness and irritation. She looked to the bathrooms at the back of the plane but they seemed so far away.

A tall flight attendant with springy brown curls put an arm on her shoulder. "Are you in first class?" he asked. "This is the first-class washroom."

Marcella shook her head slowly. "No, we have premium seats, right there," she murmured and pointed to where Matt was sitting. "I ..." she started to say, and looked away. The flight attendant's eyes lingered on her stomach. It still looked like rising dough trying to burst out of the bottom of her purple shirt. "Oh," he said quickly, "never mind. Go right ahead." Marcella raced inside. She locked the door behind her and burst into tears.

Marcella had been seventeen weeks pregnant. Pregnant enough to start telling everyone. Pregnant enough to have morning sickness, to eat too many bagels and crackers and bowls of pasta and use pregnancy as an excuse. Pregnant enough to start buying maternity clothes and thinking about having a baby all the time. Pregnant enough to spend hours online, looking at lists of baby names and imagining what it would be like to have her. Marcella had seen an obstetrician twice, but she wouldn't find out until twenty weeks whether she was having a girl or a boy. Marcella knew without a doubt that her baby was a girl. She eyed white baby dresses and pink tutus, baby running shoes, and basketball jerseys. She bought a copy of *The Paper Bag Princess*.

Somehow, when it happened, she was less shocked than she should have been.

The night before, her skin felt like it was roasting, even though it was ten below outside, and their bedroom wasn't properly heated. She ripped her clothes off and yelled at Matt for the layers of blankets he slept with. She had a nightmare about being attacked by a man on the subway. He took a knife out of his pocket and aimed for her stomach. She screamed and tried to shield herself. She tried to kick him and he stabbed her in the leg.

When she woke up, she was crying. Her leg felt bruised.

She touched her stomach. It felt like something was moving, even though she'd read that she wouldn't feel movements until later on. We're having a super baby, she thought. She tried to smile. She sat up gingerly and asked Matt to help her to get out of bed.

She saw his face turn white as he gripped her arm. "Marci," he said, "you're bleeding."

She felt the blood drip hot, down her legs. She saw it hit the floor. She sat down hard on the couch and heard Matt dial 911.

The doctors told her that there was nothing that she could have done differently.

The blood tests didn't show any anomalies. Sometimes it just happens, they kept saying.

The bleeding wouldn't stop, so she had to stay at the hospital overnight.

Matt sat in a chair next to her bed and held her hand. He asked her if she wanted him to text their families to tell them. She shook her head. "Not yet."

The next morning she had a scan that confirmed that her pregnancy sack was empty.

She stared vacantly at the screen. Everything was over, just like that.

She wasn't sure how she'd explain it to people.

Marcella wiped her eyes and went back to her seat. It kept hitting her at strange times.

The doctors told her that they could start trying again whenever she felt ready.

When the flight attendants brought lunch around, she chose lasagne. It was a tiny portion of gluey cheese and overcooked pasta, but she swallowed fast.

The one thing that hadn't gone away with the pregnancy was her appetite.

If Matt had noticed, he hadn't said anything.

* * *

Matt and Marcella had been married for almost two years, and together for seven.

They met in the second year of their MBA. Everyone kept saying how perfect they were, from their shared interests to their Italian backgrounds. Their friends called them M&M.

They decided to pool their wedding money and their savings to buy a townhouse close to Marcella's parents. They'd only been on one trip to Cuba, where they'd danced and drunk and Matt had proposed to her.

On her bucket list were Australia, Fiji and New Zealand. He wanted to go to Costa Rica. When Marcella's pregnancy test came back positive, all their friends urged them to fly off somewhere while they still could.

"Kids change everything," they said.

Marcella said what she wanted most was to travel to a beautiful beach. Miami was close but unexotic, and she was worried about COVID and all the vocal Florida antivaxxers.

One day Matt was walking past a travel agent's office that was offering honeymoon specials at half price and signed them up for two weeks in Hawaii. He was sure Marcella would love it.

"We just won't tell them when we got married," he said. "It'll still be romantic."

* * *

When they got to Honolulu, Marcella was surprised by how fancy their hotel was. Matt was the kind of guy who insisted on buying all their groceries online so he could save twenty-seven cents on a can of tuna. She was expecting a two and a half star all-inclusive resort.

Their hotel's lobby was white marble, with a twenty-foot Christmas tree covered in gold and silver lights, and a giant silver menorah standing near the reception desk. There was a wraparound patio with lounge chairs and an amazing view of the turquoise sea.

They passed a coffee shop that served acai bowls and avocado toast. The bartender eyed them as they passed. "I made virgin pina coladas if you want to try some," he said and handed them each a tiny plastic cup.

Marcella shook her head. "No, not a virgin. Make mine the real thing."

Their hotel room had an ocean view. She padded out onto the balcony and looked down at the private lagoon beach.

It was thirty-two degrees but the sky was cloudy. She came inside. A plate of strawberries had the word "congratulations" spelled out in thick white chocolate fondant. Beside it was a card with a rainbow on it. *Aloha, Dear Guests*, she read out loud. *Aloha means more than hello and goodbye. Aloha means Love, Peace, and Compassion. A life of Aloha is a life of sincerity and openness, a life where the heart is so full it is overflowing with the ability to influence others around you with your spirit.*

She stopped reading. There was a small champagne bucket with two paper thin glasses.

"I guess we can have this now," Matt said, and picked up the bottle. They heard thunder and then a light spray of rain. A rainbow peeked through the clouds as impossibly vibrant as if it had been placed there with CGI effects. She wanted to roll her eyes and tell Matt that he didn't have to try so hard. He put his hand on her arm, and she waited a whole minute before she brushed it off.

The next morning, they went downstairs for a buffet breakfast. The hotel was beside a Disney resort and the beach and the pool were crawling with kids. Marcella piled her plate with eggs and roasted potatoes and tiny red velvet pancakes.

A middle-aged server with fading red hair came to their table to get their drink orders. Marcella asked for coffee and the waitress raised her over-plucked eyebrows.

She put a hand on Marcella's shoulder. "Don't worry, we have decaf."

Marcella stared back at her. "Why would I worry?"

The server leaned in, and her silver flower necklace tickled Marcella's neck. "A few more months of not having coffee is nothing. Take it from me, I had four kids. It's better not to take the risk."

Marcella glared at Matt, but he shrugged helplessly. He had always been pathologically unable to confront anyone, to protect her. Now, she could see it in his eyebrows, in the lines around his tight smile; he pitied her. It was too much.

Matt was taken aback by her silence.

He was only capable of thinking of a great, scathing comeback hours or even days later.

The old Marcella was impossibly fast on her feet.

Matt could practically hear her response, hear it in the distant and matter of fact way she would have said it.

"Are you fat shaming me? I'm just the kind of girl who's always carried extra weight in my stomach."

They would have laughed about it afterwards.

Maybe if she felt like being more open, she would have said: "I used to be pregnant but I'm not anymore, so now I can drink whatever the fuck I want."

He would have reached for her hand and glared at the server.

He wished Marcella would just say something. She stared at the table and put her thumb in the corner of her eye. "My contacts are bothering me," she said so quietly he almost didn't hear her.

Marcella had been quieter for more than a year now, ever since she'd found out about him and Andrea. He hadn't really known how to explain himself. It wasn't just that she was pretty, and funny, that she'd recently graduated from college, with the future an amorphous sea of unrealistic possibilities. It was that she wasn't tethered to planning and achieving the painstaking details of a future together. She hadn't bet everything she had on him. She was present, she seemed to actually like him, and that was something, wasn't it?

He stopped seeing her, of course, and he even went to some counselling sessions with Marcella.

If having a kid would bring them closer, he figured, it wasn't the worst reason.

Marcella got up from the table. She told Matt she needed the bathroom but they both knew she wanted to walk alone on the boardwalk. She was grateful that he didn't try to follow her. She passed beach after beach, palm and carob trees, and pink and blue payphones that looked like they'd been found on the set of an eighties movie. Finally she came to a beach that was relatively deserted. She took her shoes off and walked towards the edge of the water.

Marcella heard a couple with their thirteen-year-old daughter approaching. As they walked behind her they made it clear to their teenager that they'd like her to do more than lie on the beach all day.

"Have you ever been paddle boarding?" the father asked.

"Like ever in my life, or on this trip?"

Marcella almost laughed out loud.

If she'd had a child with Matt, it would have taken all of her energy, and nothing she could have done would have anchored him. She was tired of being the immoveable lead around his wrists, the unspoken weight that prevented him from being impulsive.

She waved to the family as she turned back to the boardwalk. "Aloha," she muttered.

Marcella was finally sure that one day, when she had all her ducks in a row, she would leave him.

Look at Him

He said: "It's all in your head."
And I said: "So's everything." But he didn't get it.
—Fiona Apple, Paper Bag

PEOPLE HAVE ALWAYS SAID that I'm good at reading people, that I have a good sense of what they're thinking and feeling. That sensitivity is what makes me a good artist, a couple of critics have said. It's what gives my work depth. I wish those qualities were less of a liability in my personal life.

I picked this coffee chain for its neutrality. If I was deliberate and chose a place from our past, it would seem like I still had feelings beyond curiosity.

There's no home court advantage here, just the awkwardness of two artists overpaying for coffee.

He sits in a chair in the window, backlit by the sun, a half smile on his wolf in wolf's clothing face. I'm tempted to draw him, his shoulders rolled back confidently, his legs stretched out to take up the maximum amount of space.

He waves with two fingers when he sees me, and when I come closer, he locks eyes with me and gives me his hundred-watt, full intensity smile. A part of me knows he's putting it on, but his smile still makes me feel like a kid who was given an unexpected prize, a tiny toy inside a Kinder Surprise. There are new lines that crinkle in the corners of his honey molten eyes, a few grey hairs by his temples, a new tattoo peeking out from under the sleeve of his black T-shirt, and I marvel at the ridiculousness of him being more beautiful now, like a redwood that gets more sublime with age.

I sit across from him, my knees feeling the familiar electricity. I tap the table with my fingertips.

He wasn't my first boyfriend, or the person I lost my virginity to. But he was the first person who I thought might understand me. He always struck the safest balance of boundaries and openness, of deep interest and distance. It was fine until I started wanting more.

"It's good to see you," I say. And he laughs, like he knows how bizarre this is too, but here we are.

We both order coffees, his black, mine with vanilla oatmilk and sugar.

He taps the inside of my arm, gently, an opening drumbeat when the drinks come.

We talk about books we've both read recently, favourite songs that have been soundtracks to creativity. He holds up my right hand, the back of it and the underside of my arm still covered in streaks of red and yellow paint.

"*Plus ça change, plus c'est la même chose,*" I say, wondering if I've said it right and he shrugs.

"Sounds good to me," he says, even though I don't think I actually asked. I smile and look down at my hand.

I talk about my latest paintings. "I've been obsessed with bright combinations lately. Vibrant oranges and cobalt blues, ocean blue and mint green and magenta, lime green and the softest lavenders and lilacs."

He can make anyone feel like they're the most riveting person he's ever met. It's part of how he got me in the first place. There's something amazing about someone really listening to you.

He tells me about the latest movie he's producing, the story, the casting, where they're shooting it. He's as passionate as ever.

When I was in art school, there were artists infinitely more talented than me. There were people who could sculpt and whittle and make prints, people who could bead and craft and do murals. There were people who could draw from life so realistically you'd think you were looking at a photo. But there were few people who spent as many late nights in the studio as I did. There were few people who wanted to make it as badly as I did.

I introduced myself to him after seeing him around. He said I looked familiar, and I reached into my sketchbook and pulled out a drawing of him. I had no idea how he'd react but he told me he loved it.

We had so many intense conversations, ideas and words, passion and music. He always said I needed to stop apologizing for my ambitions. He always asked to see my work, the process, the finished stuff. He always asked in depth questions. The more we talked, the more time I wanted to spend with him, the more I wanted to extend every moment. I wanted to talk all night long; I wanted to know everything about him.

When we've swallowed the last dregs of our coffee we get up, walk around the old neighbourhood.

"Remember the fight we had over here," I say, nodding my head to the left of us, and first he laughs, but when he registers the hurt in my face, he stops, suddenly serious.

"It was hard, what happened with us," he said.

This surprises me because I was never sure what was in my head and what was real. It always felt like I was the one who loved and wanted more. I reach over and squeeze his hand. We both hold on for too long. He's the one who pries his fingers loose.

"There are things more painful than the way things ended between us," I say.

He looks at me, his eyes widening with irritation that he can hardly conceal, a deep breath where he tries to center himself, where he takes an actual step back, when he tries to hear me out because it's the Right Thing To Do.

I'm never good at being on the spot. I don't mean to delay, it's not a tactic, I want to say, just an anxiety disorder, and I want him to laugh, but I know he won't unless I give him explicit permission to, which would make all of this superfluous.

"It's worse," I find myself saying quietly, "to know that you never fully had someone. To know that the spark, the potential for real happiness was there ..."

I hear him take a deep breath. I wonder if he'll walk away now, but he doesn't move, and I continue.

"It's worse to know that you occupy no space in a person's heart or mind, a person you thought about all the time."

"No," he says, and puts his arms around me. He always gave the best hugs, hugs that pull your whole body into his, the kind that can somehow be both reassuring and sensual, the kind that leave you both standing there for too long, and when you cross the street and look away, he's still looking back at you, intensely.

He says something into my hair. I think he says something about it not being true, and I say something into his shoulder, something like it is true, because if it wasn't you would have been in touch before this, you would have let me know and he shakes his head, and I know this is as close as I'm going to get to him admitting anything. I run my hand along his cheek like I used to.

I want to kiss him, and I think he wants to kiss me too, but that was always the problem. I was never sure how much I was imagining and how much was real. I think about a line in a poem I read a long time ago, about a kiss in someone's eyes that haunts the poet.

"I could continue being happy for you from a distance," I say, "but this is good, seeing you, hearing everything you've been up to now."

He nods. "It is good," he says, and looks down.

He says something about how he always knew I'd do the things I was doing now, and I say it to him too, and I think we both mean it.

There was always something in the way. It was work, or life, a hidden partner with a complicated history. Most of all I think it was fear, but maybe as much as it hurt at the time, maybe none of the reasons matter. Maybe that's what makes it easier now to say the right things, to turn away when I feel tears coming, to give him one last hug, to feel his eyes on my back as I walk away even though I've been too afraid to turn around and look at him.

A Good Story to Tell

We met at a Shakshuka bar on our town's main street. He was from a small city just north of us, the same place we went to for school supplies and shoes before our town had its own mall. Our town banned heavy industry, and the mall was in an area we called "the industrial zone" though all it had aside from the mall was a bakery, a clothing outlet, and two massive grocery stores.

Before that, there were the shops and restaurants on the main street that often changed within two years, and a tiny movie theatre on the other side of town.

Everyone knew the Shakshuka bar wouldn't last. It took a classic, takes five minutes to make it at home dish and made it fancy and expensive. There's nothing people around here hate more than feeling like they're being ripped off.

Seriously, you open a can of tinned tomatoes, throw them in a frying pan, add some spices, a tiny bit of honey if the tomatoes are acidic, throw in some eggs, cook on low heat, and there you go. Microwave some pita to eat on the side. Take some hummus out of the fridge. The end.

This place added greens and kale and feta cheese and olives and shallots and mushrooms and all kind of abominable things, and yet my best friend loved it. She found it sophisticated and interesting, and she offered to pay for me, so here we were.

Hila was technically my third cousin. To her all food was conceptual. She liked, in her words "*li'tom hakol*," to taste everything. I was the opposite. I could easily devour things whole, mindlessly and constantly. I had to remind myself to chew and force myself to stop.

I was all instinct; I liked to experience first and analyze after. She liked to be deliberate and measured. She took so much pride in self control I thought it was ridiculous, but I still loved her and even grudgingly admired her sometimes.

When we were kids it was always me who got into trouble. Hila had the best poker face even when we were five. Her name meant halo and adults would see her blonde wavy hair and bright yellow dresses and believe anything she said. I felt guilty before we'd done anything.

We were both artists. I played violin when we were younger, and she danced ballet and modern. When we were older, I played guitar, and sang and wrote songs, and she painted.

Neither of us liked anything trendy, so we went to the Shakshuka place as a joke but then she started to love it.

Her favourite dish was the *Shakshuka Parmigiana*, which was full of mozzarella, eggplant, and parmesan, along with the usual things. I once ordered what I thought was normal Shakshuka, but it was full of tiny chili peppers, and I accidentally ate two whole. After crying in the bathroom, not sure if I was seeing chili peppers, tomatoes or blood, she made me promise we didn't have to go back.

I was surprised when Omri wanted to go there on our first date. Hila had mentioned it once, so he assumed I loved it too.

We met two weeks before, at a house party. A few days later he showed up at Hila's apartment, where we were lounging on the balcony. I figured either they were good friends, or he liked her. Guys always liked Hila, and it wasn't just because she was pretty. It was because she didn't give a shit about any of them. She'd ignore them completely, or fix them with a withering stare, her eyes frozen jade, her long, dark blonde eyelashes fluttering prettily as her lips said fuck off, and they'd compete for her attention. I was the opposite. I saw infinite possibilities in all of them, their talent, their humour, their potential sweetness and sensitivity. I could have fallen in love with any of them, on any day, so I tried to hold myself back.

It turned out Omri was there for me. He offered to walk me home, and the next thing I knew he was kissing me, his teeth scraping my bottom lip. His parents were out of town the next weekend so he invited me over. I was on birth control, not because I was regularly sexually active but because my skin was a mess without it. I wasn't scheduled to get my period that day, but I did, and the next thing I knew the sheets on his single bed were stained symmetrically like rose petals but he said he didn't mind.

He was gentle until he took off his pants. He told me he'd had other superficial girlfriends who cared about things like size, which was crazy because he could do anything a bigger guy could do, and he was generous and eager to show me when my cycle was over.

I stared at him, his thick, dark eyebrows knitted into an upward arrow, his brown eyes darting all over the room. "Omri, I like you," I found myself saying, even though I wasn't sure how much or why.

He kept calling and texting after that.

My cousin told him I was a musician and that I sang and wrote songs, and then he wouldn't leave me alone. He constantly begged to hear my music.

I demurred because nothing good ever comes of revealing yourself fully when you somehow know that you shouldn't trust them.

He told me that he wrote his own songs and offered to show me his lyrics. We'll do an even trade, one day, I told him, and then Hila sent him two of my songs.

One was a song that I'd written for a national contest. I'd won second place. She also sent him a song she said she could imagine on the radio. It was loud and heavy, and sounded amazing with a full band. I recorded them in an expensive studio in Tel Aviv. I worked for two months in a shoe store to pay for three days in the studio, including musicians and production. Still it was the most fun I'd ever had.

The songs were written in my living room, because it had the best acoustics. I had to find the times when no one else was home, when it was just me, my guitar and my voice filling up the space.

If you asked me what my dreams were, and I was feeling open right then, I might have said: I wanted to play to crowds. I had a vision of playing at festivals, seeing hundreds or even thousands of people dancing and swaying and singing back my words. My music made me feel connected to all of them, like a place where we all belonged.

I didn't want to work in an ordinary job. I didn't even want to go to college. I wanted to get paid to spend hours every day writing and creating.

I was always aware of my limitations. I had an emotive voice but not a five octave classically trained one.

I'd studied guitar for years but my piano skills were very basic. I wrote too many songs in minor keys. I didn't know how to write about happy things. I never, ever felt cool.

Still, I wanted to be a musician more than anything.

I felt at home in the studio and on stage.

We went back to the Shakshuka Café that night. I ordered the Parmigiana again, because it contained no surprises. We got through all of dinner without him mentioning my songs. I didn't think I cared that much about what he thought, but I found myself asking him in a little girl voice I didn't recognize if he liked them.

He looked at me, anger clouding his features.

"*At Rotza Lefarsem*," he said, you want to become famous. "I thought you cared about art, and music, but …"

He didn't finish the sentence and I sat there quietly, pushing my food around, hoping he'd still pay for it.

"It's hard to explain," he said when we walked out of the restaurant. "When you look at Hila, and her paintings, it's art for art's sake."

I wanted to scream. His assumption that I wasn't a real artist, that I didn't put thought and ideas and emotion into every word, that he didn't know me or see me hurt the most.

I thought about all the songs that changed my life, the way my hands and knees shook when I got to meet my favourite musicians and singers. I dreamed that one day someone would feel like that about something I wrote and I'd know that I was here for a reason.

"You're right," I said to him slowly. "I do want people to hear my songs. I do want people to like them. I want people see me."

I started to cry, and he reached an arm out but I pushed him away.

I cried all the way to Hila's house, thinking how unfair it was that our friends who worked hard to develop apps or small businesses, or who went to university were considered ambitious, but if you worked hard in the arts, people thought you were naïve.

"It'll be a good story to tell," she said quietly, when I got there, my face pink and tear streaked, and she pulled me into a tight hug. "When you're famous, and you're doing interviews, and they ask you about your early days, you can talk about this guy who was stupid enough not to support you. And the interviewer will look at you and laugh and shake his head and say what a fucking idiot. I bet he regrets it now. And you'll look at him, all generous and loving, like you always do, and you'll say something like we just weren't right for each other, and you won't expect it to feel good. because it was so long ago, but you will feel better, just hearing that reaction."

Later that night, I found myself sitting outside my apartment building so I wouldn't wake up my family, plucking at my guitar strings, as angry lyrics poured out of me. I called it "Mr. Index Finger," and it had a chorus that went "accusing me/ pointing it in my face/ treating my ambition like some kind of disgrace." I imagined it playing on rock and even pop music stations, girls sharing stories with me backstage. I imagined myself feeling confident, maybe finding someone who would understand, and even support me in wanting to be myself. I imagined the interview Hila talked about. As I walked inside, I started to feel a little bit better.

Ellipsis

His name was Kobe—"like Kobe Bryant," he said—and I shuddered because I'd never known anything about basketball except the celebrity headlines, like Kobe's cheating scandal. I looked at his pale eyes, the perfect shade between sky and ocean and thought of the purple diamond that Kobe Bryant gifted his wife after the other woman went public. I could've walked away, the room was packed with other staff, included my roommate Alexis. I glanced over at her, and she grinned, her blonde eyebrows slightly quizzical. She was, as always, surrounded by boys, a British guy and two Israelis were trying to test her Hebrew vocabulary, and she was laughing, flashing her perfectly symmetrical teeth, freckles on her nose jumping as if every single part of her found them hilarious.

"I like Kobe beef," I said, and he laughed.

"That's the one from Japan, right?"

I nodded. "*Nir'ah li*," I said, I think so.

"I read that they massage those cows, that's what gives them the flavour."

"What?"

"They massage them with sake. Seriously, look it up."

I turned away and started walking towards the door. "I will," I said, and then like an idiot, I added: "Lucky cows. I love massages."

He started walking behind me. "Me too," he said. "It could totally make me forget I was about to be someone's dinner."

I'd let someone eat me if I got a great massage first, I thought, then realized I'd said it out loud.

He blushed and I stared down at my neon orange Converse, another sign that screamed that I was a foreigner, despite my nearly perfect Hebrew.

I felt his hand on my elbow. "I give great massages, Roni," he said, and then he disappeared into his cubicle.

I'd met him a few weeks before, along with everyone else. Ostensibly, they hired us all because we were bilingual. The job paid surprisingly well.

We had shockingly little training. They gave us a book of facts about American citizenship, and the extremely slim odds of actually winning a green card, which is what we promised people could possibly happen if they paid us a fee, gave us their passport number and filled in some forms. They also gave us a brief talk about who would call us and why they so badly wanted to leave the country. It's weird when you're trying hard to settle in and build a life, to earn money from people who want do the exact opposite.

Most of them were at least twenty-five. They'd finished their army service, travelled to India or Thailand or South America and realized that what they couldn't do was come back and live here.

For some, it was ideological. Having been forced to serve in the army, after watching their parents drive with guns in their cars, their dads or brothers constantly called for reserve duty, and more than a handful of dead relatives and friends, they wanted an easier life, or a life with a cleaner conscience. Some said they didn't want to put their own kids through it. Others said it came from experiencing life in other countries and realizing that it didn't have to be this way, despite what they'd been told their whole lives.

For a handful it was about education, wanting to do master's or PhD in the U.S., wanting more job security, working and living in a completely first world country, where small things like bureaucracy and basic customer service weren't massive battles.

I already knew the list because I'd heard them all from my parents.

My parents were Israelis who moved to Vancouver when I was nine. My dad worked in IT, and my mom became the Jewish studies vice principal of the local Jewish day school, so my sister Orly and I went to school there. When you move from another country to Israel, people call it making *Aliya*, which means going up. When you leave Israel, they call it *Yerida*, as if inevitably life anywhere else could only be a downward spiral.

As if you deserve to have friends who ask you if you're a 'Jewy Jew', who lightly say that Jews talk about the Holocaust too much, who ask for proof, who joke that Jews don't have ethics.

My parents couldn't believe that both my sister and I wanted to go back. They thought we just needed to toughen up, to appreciate what we had here. Once after our dad called us spoiled, my sister printed off a pile of articles about the history of the Musqueam, the Squamish, and the Tsleil-Waututh.

She tried to bring it up with him later. "We have privilege, *Abba*, but at what cost?"

But he shook his head.

"*Ein li Koach*," he said, I don't have the strength to get into this with you.

My sister, with her brilliant grades, got into a bunch of dental schools, including Tel Aviv University. They still thought she'd lost her mind, but at least it was a good profession. I finished a useless degree in Communications and took her up on the offer to crash on her couch. I didn't know what else to do, and it was kind of fun to shock and piss off my parents for the first time in my life.

It was Orly's idea to pad my resume. She had always had a talent for making questionable things sound legitimate. Even though she complained about the heat, and the interfering people, and the bad customer service more than anyone, she somehow convinced our parents that she was happy and thriving. The truth was, it was about a guy. She met Avishai on some app, and the next thing I knew, she was upending her life, without actually having met him, and as far as my parents still understood, she met him in here, dental school. The funny part is that he's in school to be a physiotherapist.

Alexis and I met at the orientation. She was a professional, nationally ranked squash player in her home country of New Zealand. She met an Israeli guy who was travelling post army. They fell in love, and she agreed to travel to the Middle East to live with him and his crazy family, who hated her on sight because she wasn't Jewish.

One day, she told me that she just couldn't take another day of living with his parents. Orly moved in with Avishai. I took her bedroom, and I gifted Alexis the couch.

Her boyfriend, Tzachi, was tall, and heavyset, with a thick, bare line curving through one of his black eyebrows from some fight. She was always complaining about how roughly he handled her, how he'd push her out of bed, or out their bedroom door, to make breakfast for his family.

I mentioned it to Kobe one day, as we stood outside after work.

"I don't get it. She's so beautiful, and smart."

He looked up at me, the sun turning his eyes into pale, shiny aquamarines. He squinted and put his hands over his forehead.

"You think she's smart?"

I shrugged. "You don't?"

"Imagine giving up everything, your life, a legitimate career, your family, for a guy like Tzachi."

I shook my head. I didn't say that I thought she was brave, or that at least now Alexis would never look back and wonder what if.

Kobe was quieter than the other guys I worked with, who loudly hit on any woman with a pulse. He shrugged when I mentioned this later.

"My parents are Americans," he said, as if Americans were the most well mannered, civilized people on earth. They were from Seattle. He still had relatives there, and we figured out that when we were eleven, we both visited Whistler at the same time. Some of his American cousins called him Jake, since Kobe was short for Yaacov, or Jacob in English, and I told him about some of my Canadian friends asking if Roni was short for Veronica, and how I told them it was, because it was easier. That's who we were from now on, he said, Veronica and Jake. Sometimes in texts he called me Veronica. Sometimes I called him Jake and sometimes I called him Archie. For Purim a few weeks later, when our bosses made us dress up for work, he dyed his hair red with a washable spray, and let me draw freckles on him with brown eyeliner, and I bought a long black wig, and wore piles of Alexis's jewellery and one of her short skirts.

We didn't talk about our dating history in much detail. In my second year of university, I slept with two guys, one because I liked him, the other because I just wanted the night to end. In Israel, where everyone was open with their feelings and their bodies, it was easier get swept up, and I did, with two more guys and a woman. The experiences weren't bad, but they weren't as great as I'd expected either. I wanted sex to feel more urgent and meaningful.

Alexis told me I had to stop dressing like a little girl. She went through my closet and tossed all my long skirts and harem pants. I tried on some of her clothes, her shorts, her low-cut tank tops, but our bodies were different. She had abs where I had stomach fat and I didn't feel like myself.

Kobe told me about a girlfriend he had with whom he travelled from India to Thailand. She was so tiny, and light that she would walk across his back every night before bed. She was better than any masseuse, he said. He mentioned that he'd gone on a date with Shoshi, one of our coworkers, when he first started working there, over a year before. She had wild, curly brown hair and worked part time as a Pilates instructor.

I asked her about dating him once and she waved a beige manicured hand. "It never went beyond coffee," she said. "He's a nice guy, but he's weird." She paused and laughed her deep, one of the guys, laugh. "Kind of you like you."

I wasn't sure if it was a compliment or an insult.

Alexis and I invited everyone over after work one night. We dug into the bottles of wine that my sister always kept on hand and ordered pizza. Everyone came, even Kobe. We stood around awkwardly until he pulled out a chair for me and started giving me a neck massage. I closed my eyes and smiled.

"This feels amazing," I said after a few minutes.

He leaned over me. "*Amarti lach*," he said. "I told you."

He left two hours earlier than everyone else and asked me to walk him to his car. We'd had a little to drink, and I leaned in to give him a hug and he bent down, his full bottom lip quivering before he leaned in and kissed me. Tiny white flowers from the kumquat hedge beside us got caught in his hair, and I pulled them out. I ran a finger along his sharp cheekbones. He smiled at me, like he was taking all of me in, as if he really liked what he saw. I ran up the five flights of stairs to our apartment, full of new energy.

After that, he'd give me massages in the staff room, in front of people, or asked me to give him one, or referenced things that we'd talked about, just me and him. I knew everyone assumed there was something going on, but the worst part was that there wasn't really. He'd drive me home from work sometimes or accompany me on errands ranging from buying fresh pita to playing with the puppies in a nearby pet store. He'd shrug with the affectionate reluctance of a boyfriend, raising his arms to our coworkers, like *what can I do, it's what the lady wants*.

I thought about asking him on a real date. I thought about things he liked to do for fun, like playing volleyball, or watching soccer games. His team was Hapoel Tel Aviv and when we went to watch a game once I fell asleep on his shoulder. He wouldn't let me live it down.

He didn't like movies or music that much. He knew that I liked my coffee iced, with three percent milk and no sugar. Sometimes we sat in his car, him drinking water, or hot black coffee, holding hands, discussing stupid things, like why the words for *nikui yavesh* were dry cleaning in English, and whatever stupid thing our boss had done that day. One night after making out in his car, in full view of my neighbours, I begged him to come upstairs. I flinched when he turned his body away from me. He reached over and kissed my forehead. "Not yet," he said.

I tried again a few nights later. He kissed me back this time and shook his head.

"It's too soon."

I thought that feeling this way was what I'd wanted, but it's embarrassing to want someone so much. I didn't know what to do with myself.

I tried to focus on finding a new job, and on making new friends,

Maybe it was because he felt me drifting away, but Kobe became a little more attentive. He said that my green shirt made my eyes look more intense. He ran his fingers through my hair one night as I lay with my head on his lap, looking up at him. "You're so beautiful, Roni," he said, and I wanted these moments to be enough but they weren't.

My neighbour Tomer asked me out, and even though I was sure I didn't like him, I slept with him. I closed my eyes, I pretended he was Kobe. He was nowhere near as tender, I wanted it in a way I never had.

He came with me to a work party and introduced himself to Alexis and some of our friends as my new boyfriend.

Kobe looked like I'd punched him when Tomer said hi to him, his arm draped around me. He stared at the ground and avoided eye contact. I tried to catch up with him after the party, but he pretended he didn't hear me and walked away. After that, he avoided my texts, and never answered my WhatsApp messages, even the stupid ones that were full of nothing but Gifs and inside jokes.

Eventually, I got a job I actually wanted at an advertising firm.

Alexis finally left Tzachi for an Israeli musician and all three of us danced and partied at Orly and Avishai's wedding.

Seeing them dancing made me realize that, even though it had been more than a year, I still missed Kobe. I still thought about him all the time.

I texted him that night to tell him I missed him but he didn't answer.

I know he read the letter that I wrote him at four in the morning, when I'd drunk too much and slid into his DM's. I thanked him for helping me to open my heart. I told him that I thought I'd loved him, at the time, and now I was sure, and that whatever happened, I hoped that he was happy.

The next day, I saw the three dots appear on his text when I showed it to Alexis. They disappeared and vanished five or six times, and I knew there was something he wanted to say, but he couldn't bring himself to say it.

Black Market Encounters

OFFICIALLY, our group is called Black Market Encounters. Once, our psychiatrist jokingly called us the Meet Brute Club; another time, the Dead Wives Club. We're a support group for people who met their partners in socially unacceptable ways. The average person has a low threshold for our kinds of stories, unless it's to champion the poor aggrieved wife, and agree about how awful we are. It's not even that we cared, more that at a certain point, most of us wanted normal things, friends, people understood us and didn't judge us.

This is where Dr. Marcus Black came in. He found us online, through a survey. He pays us to be here, because, he says, that's how important we are to his research. He says he wants to prove, definitively, that monogamy is nothing more than a social construct.

He provides us with snacks and drinks, crackers and brie, sugar free candy and wine, and "a safe place to air our grievances and connect with others who've engaged in similar but reasonable patterns of behaviour."

We meet once a week in his plush, multi leather sofa-ed, charcoal grey carpeted office. In the past, most of us would have laughed at the idea of needing a safe space, but his voice is comforting, and having him sit there, taking notes, telling us that what we thought or felt was understandable was such a balm. The truth gave us back a bit of our former selves. I've actually made new friends, which Andrew thinks is great, and that's really something, since he's totally anti-therapy.

When I meet people I don't know, I just say I met my husband through work.

What I normally don't say is I'm a midwife, and I met him when I was helping to deliver his then wife's baby.

Andrew and I lived in the same neighbourhood. We frequented the same artisanal doughnuts, the same pet store (we're both cat people) and the same LCBO. We could have met reaching for the same organic salmon treats for the cats we were each fostering, for the same cat rescue downtown.

I'd been a doula for five years before I decided to become licensed as a midwife. When I met Andrew, I was almost fully certified, but I was still assisting the main midwife on call. He wasn't often there, and when he was, he was visibly anxious, fiddling with his pale fingers, and pacing back and forth. I registered his penetrating blue eyes, and his tousled, dishwater blond hair.

You meet two types of husbands as a midwife. There's the kind who breathe heavily and tell you that they'd be the ones carrying the baby themselves if they could, and they sweat, holding their wives' hands, doing breathing exercises, complaining that they're exhausted.

Then there's the hands-off kind, who volunteer to take care of the other kids, or run every possible errand. If they're there, they're reading books or articles, asking questions that imply that they know more than us.

Andrew wasn't trying to prove how devoted he was, and he wasn't condescending towards us either. He was terrified.

I wasn't surprised when he told me that the baby hadn't been planned. He'd never wanted to have kids, and Angie, who'd never said so outright, always had. He'd asked her to marry him, he said, after four years of dating, because she was getting restless.

The name Angelina suited her. She was a Pre-Raphaelite red haired beauty, with smooth, milky skin and a gap between her front teeth that stopped her from looking too perfect.

Her birth plan included blasting the David Bowie and Queen song "Under Pressure," followed by "Fruits of My Labour" by Lucinda Williams if it was going well, and "The Drugs Don't Work" by the Verve if it wasn't. Still, she couldn't hide the unadulterated joy that snuck into her eyes as she got closer to giving birth. Occasionally, excitement overtook him too, but he always whispered it to me, not her. Suzanna, the more experienced midwife, looked at me oddly when I told her what I'd observed.

"Why do you care so much?" she said. "Let's just focus on the baby."

I tried to support Angie, but she shrugged me off. "It's good that there's two of you," she said. "Go see if Andrew needs anything."

What do you do when a woman throws her husband at you at the exact moment when they should be bonding? As per her request, I spent most of my time with him. It was her first pregnancy, so it went on for twenty-seven hours, and we had time to sit in their kitchen, drinking terrible coffee. We talked and talked. When his daughter was born, and Angelina told me her name was Allegra, because she made her so happy, Andrew motioned for me to follow him into the backyard. We stood next to the red plastic baby swing he'd put up. It was too dark to see any stars. He leaned me against the brick wall, careful not to set off their motion detector, and kissed me. I looked up and the moon hung above us like a thin sliver of hope. We'd been awake for almost forty-eight hours and everything felt like a dream. I looked down at my wrinkled green scrubs, felt my hair bursting out of its ponytail. I was fifteen years younger than him. When Angie went back to work after a month I joined him to babysit whenever I could. He took six months of paternity leave. Andrew was a better father than either of us expected. When Allegra napped, and she napped a lot, for three to four hours at a stretch, Andrew and I made love and made plans for the future. I didn't really believe it until he told her he was leaving her for me. Allegra had just turned one. Angie lost her shit, crying and screaming, eyeliner smeared like an emo kid from the 2000's. But after we got married, and now that I'm pregnant, she's calmed down a little. She still refuses to call me Allegra's stepmom. I started getting more emotional in my second trimester, which is when I found Dr. Black.

It's such a relief to tell people how much I wanted him and the life we have now. I do feel guilty, if I let myself think about it but as my friend Alexis from the group says: "How can you feel bad if something you did lead to everything you've always wanted?"

Maybe Andrew and I were just meant to be.

One night Andrew and Alexis' boyfriend Cole bonded in the parking lot when they were both there to pick us up.

Like Alexis has a caregiving job. She works as a behaviour specialist with autistic kids. Cole was one of her client's fathers. She said she'd never seen such a dedicated, hands-on dad. Until then she'd mostly dealt with moms.

"I couldn't pick his ex out of a line up. I literally never saw her. Cole drove Jesse and picked him up every single day. He'd call me and want to hear about every part of his day. Jesse is such a smart and sweet boy, we really bonded. Cole always looked so exhausted, because the kid was always up all night, and he was the one staying up with him."

It happened gradually, she explained. She or Cole would text each other just to say hi. She found after-school programs for Jesse, and celebrated with Cole when they went well. Their first kiss was in the parking lot, while they were waiting for another therapist to bring Jesse outside. They had sex in the backseat of his car a couple of weeks later. He told her he hadn't had sex in two years. Not long after, he left his wife and Alexis started working at a different support center. His ex-wife said that Alexis had all the sensitivity of a robot, even as a therapist, which bothered Alexis, and Cole had to remind her that she didn't really know her.

Alexis found out about Dr. Black through her friend Kaylee, who was a former nanny to the stars. The dad was a famous hockey player and the mom was a reality TV star. She was one of three nannies for their two kids. The wife hired her, and they got along great. She took her shopping, gifted her with her old designer handbags and jewellery, and overpaid her. One day, she led her to their giant walk-in closet, gave her a twenty-four-carat gold dildo, dropped her pants and showed her how to use it. Soon, they were having sex regularly, and when her husband came back, they had their first threesome. They called her their sex toy, and it happened a few more times until they fired her with a generous severance package and a seven-page long NDA.

There was Kathleen the teacher, who'd slept with two teenage boys. Kathleen had confessed through her lawyer and had a very short prison sentence. It was hard to imagine her in jail. She had perfect posture, wavy brown hair, and green eyes that she hid behind rimless, nerdy glasses. She looked and acted older than twenty-five. She didn't like the rest of our jokes, made faces when we swore and refused to drink with us. The boy was sixteen and lived with his aunt and uncle. His mom had died was he was a little kid. He wore a Beatles T-shirt to class one day, and they connected. "He's an old soul," she said. His name was Avi. The fact that they were still in touch was something we all swore we'd never repeat to anyone.

There were other less interesting stories; a daycare owner who fell in love with a married mom, who left her wife for her; a marriage counsellor who slept with some of the husbands but insisted they stay in their marriages.

The person everyone talked about most was Kendra. Kendra had been an oncology nurse. Her job was her life's work, but everything changed when she met Isabella and Darion. Isabella was only twenty-eight and had stage three lymphoma. She was beautiful and in shape, a grade one teacher who ran half marathons for charity every year. Her room was always full of balloons, stuffed animals and cards signed in messy crayons by eager, uncertain little hands. Her husband Darion had sleek, wavy hair, a generous smile and gentle eyes. He was a children's rights advocate. He liked to bake. He'd drop off homemade cookies every day at the nurse's station. Her favourites were his traditional coconut drops, a family recipe that he said took him back to Trinidad with every bite. Kendra was supposed to tell him that Isabella was getting incrementally better, but she didn't. She gave Isabella intravenous antihistamines to make her drowsy during the day, with lots of Tramadol which she told her was for the pain, but it added to Isabella's confusion. She gave her Propofol to knock her out all night. Sometimes Isabella barely recognized Darion. Kendra told him to prepare himself for the worst. Darion and Kendra used to meet after her shifts and walk around the parking lot together. One early morning they held hands and he gripped her so hard her knuckles turned white. Isabella, in one of her few lucid moments, had told him that if she didn't make it, she wanted her to move on and marry someone he could have kids with.

Darion kissed Kendra and ran his fingers through her hair for the first time. Kendra cancelled shifts to spend more time with him and one of her colleagues dropped in at her apartment to see her and caught them. Isabella got better, Darion never talked to her again and she lost her job and her license.

On what was supposed to be our last session, Dr. Black was dressed more formally, in a suit instead of jeans and a white polo shirt.

He passed out a questionnaire. It started with asking us to rank ourselves from zero to three, on statements about loyalty and empathy, and relationships, and our current partners. Then there were questions about how we saw ourselves. He looked them over in front of us, thanking us for helping him with his research. He'd used pseudonyms, he went on, but we were his featured anecdotes. He asked us how we characterized ourselves, and someone raised her hand and said determined. There was a murmur of approval, and someone else said that we were fearless romantics. Alexis said we were brave.

"I think," said Kendra in her slow, slightly paranoid cadence, "that you were studying us to determine if we have some kind of disorder."

People started shifting uncomfortably.

He confirmed it, but I could barely hear him over everyone's voices.

"I can't believe this," I heard someone saying.

"There are certain people who won't admit who they are, even to themselves. I needed access. Once you out people, they almost always run away …" he said, and I shuddered.

"We should sue you …" Kathleen said. "You lied to us. You used us."

"Ladies, these conditions are spectrums, so if you believe what I've observed to be true, it's a question of severity," he said it gently but it was a cold comfort.

He tapped on my shoulder so gently I hardly felt it.

"Aurora, you actually ranked lower than I originally expected."

I let his diagnoses sink in.

Narcissistic personality disorder. Sociopathic personality disorder.

I glared at him, willing him to feel guilty. He just shrugged back.

"I feel deceived," I said, and he shrugged, a half-smile hiding behind his beard.

As I stood outside with Alexis, her hands shaking as she tried to light her cigarette, we heard Kendra come up behind us.

"Can you believe this guy?" she asked us, and we shook our heads.

She leaned in so close we could smell her sandalwood rose perfume.

"Don't worry," she whispered. "I've got enough drugs left to make this the dead psychiatrist's club. If not, I know people who can help us."

We stared at her black puffy coat until she disappeared into the night.

When You Play with Fire

SHE HAS SKIN like two percent milk, and blonde highlighted hair. She sits in class, swimming in expensive, designer looking tan sweaters with horses on them, smiling a lot.

Her name is equally non-descript: Melissa. She used to go by Missy, she told everyone, but now she goes by Mel. Mel Schote, which if you say it fast enough sounds just like milquetoast.

If she has any of the same worries as me, about her weight, or where her next dollar is going to come from, or how to pay rent and eat, or avoid smelling like pit stains and mildew, she doesn't show it.

I don't know what grates on me, most, her casual wealth, her bland people pleasing personality or the fact that she keeps telling me she admires me. I hear the awe in her voice and it makes me want to whack her in the face with my camera lens.

Every creative genius has at least one person they can't stand. Roxane Gay is constantly tweeting about hers. Travis Shaffer did a whole photo series called Nemesis.

People think that love makes the world go round, but let me tell you, creatively speaking, the opposite is true.

Revenge and a desire to prove idiots wrong makes great art.

I get to our studio class early one day and hear her complaining about having imposter syndrome to our TA. I stifle a laugh.

I hear her say: "Look at Toni's work. It's so detailed and beautiful. She's so beautiful and accomplished."

The TA, a guy whose sweet, perplexed expression always reminds me of Charlie Brown moments after the football gets snatched from under him, tells her it's okay. "Antonella has a lot of experience. Don't compare yourself to her. She got mentored by Joseph Kowalski last summer."

"Wow. How'd she manage that?"

"Unbridled enthusiasm and talent. I don't think she was born into connections."

"I mean, I wasn't either," she started to whine.

I coughed and came up behind her.

I was wearing my hair down with my purple plastic orchid tucked behind my right ear, because Charlie Brown had told me he loved it once.

"Hi Antonella," he said, looking startled. He always gets flustered around me, which I find adorable.

I gave him my best, "oh you" eyelash bat. I never give anyone my full smile because my teeth look like uneven rows of yellowing Peruvian corn, all different shades of not white.

"How did you think I got the internship, Mel?" I asked, spitting out her name like a watermelon seed.

I rolled my eyes and made my right hand into a fist and mimed giving a blow job to Charlie.

He blushed, which made him seem even cuter.

"I didn't think that," she said, her blue eyes widening. "I would never assume that."

I snorted. Of course not. She's as pure as the cleanly fallen snow, which is why she never has any original or interesting ideas.

"I worked hard. No one's ever handed me shit." She keeps staring at me, and Charlie is standing there awkwardly, looking down, and occasionally glancing up at me, his thick eyebrows raised, and I feel a speech coming on.

The class is filing in behind them, and I feel good, knowing everyone's eyes are on me.

"It's not complicated," I say. "I've always known what I wanted to be, which is someone who captures life. Someone who shows it the way it really is. Someone who tells the truth. When my mom left my dad and me, she left one thing behind: her camera. I was so angry with her for a while, until I realized she'd given me the greatest gift, her camera and her love of photography. Well, that and my Italian citizenship." I stopped for a minute and laughed, registered a couple of my classmates laughing awkwardly behind me.

"My dad's a Turkish immigrant, right? He always says what do I know about art, Toni *balim?* But he does know. He knows about pathos. He knows about struggle. He knows about being progressive, about marrying a Catholic woman instead of a Muslim one. He knows about being proud of who he is. That's what I was capturing in my series, the apartment we moved to in Scarborough after my mom left us, the neighbourhood, the restaurants, the hidden graffiti, the tree next door. You can't fake depth or a life that's meaningful. People think cameras lie, but they expose everything."

I took a breath, and a few of my classmates started clapping. Charlie ushered me to my seat but not before I took a bow. "Thanks for coming to my TED Talk," I said.

Milquetoast came up after class to tell me I did a good job. She told me a few people had filmed it and uploaded it on their socials.

We walked together in the direction of the campus restaurants.

I wasn't surprised when she offered to pay for me. I tried to thank her, but she shrugged me off.

"It's nothing," she said.

Money always seems like nothing, unless you don't have it, I wanted to say but I bit my tongue and ordered more.

"I feel like I know a celebrity," she said, and I laughed and flicked my hair back.

"A lot of people had said that before," I said.

I checked my email when we were sitting together, when she was rambling on about her latest photo collage. It was a mix of her childhood homes, first in London and then in Israel and now her family's home in a lush, manicured suburb north of Toronto.

I wanted to tell her to call it Colonial Dreams, or My Life in Isra-hell but I didn't. She pressed me on all the things I thought she could do or change, and I shrugged. I didn't want to waste my energy.

"Do you think there's anything good about it?" she asked me in a little girl voice.

I clicked on the email from the photo festival and found out I had a photo that was going to be in it. My head swam; it was a big, national festival. Thousands of people were going to see it. This was huge. I couldn't wait to update my website and my socials. I flashed her the most generous smile I could.

"Your photos are very potent," I told her.

She smiled and looked at me, like she was waiting for more, but I couldn't hold it in anymore.

I told her what a huge deal this festival was, that they hardly ever let students be part of it, it was all professionals, and now I was one of them, officially. I wondered for a minute if she'd be one of those people who was jealous of me, who didn't want to be my friend because of all my success. It had happened before.

She blinked at me and smiled. "Mazel tov," she said.

"Are you Jewish?" I asked her, getting ready to explain about cultural appropriation. Because I was white passing, I was about to tell her, and mixed, people often made the wrong assumptions.

"Of course," she said and laughed. "Why, were you expecting me to wear a giant Star of David, maybe have a menorah in my back pocket?"

I shook my head. "I worked on a Holocaust exhibit last summer. It was amazing, we got to travel to Poland to see the camps in real life. I've never cried like I cried at Auschwitz. Are your grandparent's survivors?"

She shook her head. "No, I was lucky, my mom's parents escaped to England just before the war started," she said. "My dad's had lived there for years before."

I tried not to show my disappointment.

"That's lucky," I said.

"I know," she answered. "Believe me."

We got into a pattern of hanging out after class.

I told her what my photos of women and measuring tapes were really about.

I told her about my mom's eating disorder, the way she blamed her big thighs for my dad's cheating, the way I heard her voice in my head every time I grocery shopped or ate in a restaurant.

I told her how angry I was that my mom had remarried rich and had so much money now.

I told her how much I loved Steven Meisel, and all his photos in Madonna's sex book, how I loved Helmut Newton and his bondage photos.

I told her how hard it was that other girls were jealous of me.

The other day in class, I was wearing a tube top, and Charlie was checking me out so much, I had to tell him loudly to stop staring at my boobs.

One of the girls rolled her eyes, and another one snorted and told me to get over myself, but I knew what I saw.

I called them "flat chested asexual freaks" and Melissa laughed and laughed.

I told her about how I'd been bullied when I was in elementary school. I told her how kids called me fat, how they asked me how I could ever believe I was special. I told her about the girl who said I had a face not even a mom could love, and how much that hurt because my mom had just left. I told her how I still spend money I don't have on make up, on looking glamourous and as good as I can so that maybe she'll visit or want to see me more now that I've grown up and I'm prettier.

I even told her I'd only had sex for the first time recently, but I planned to have a lot more lovers.

She always listened. She never talked about herself, just petted my arm and told me I was beautiful and talented.

I thought I'd finally found a real friend until I saw her final project. It was called Blinded by the Spotlight.

It was portrait after portrait of me. Her artist statements were full of my personal stories. It wasn't displayed on the classroom walls or in the student gallery, but Charlie saw them and our professor saw them and I was livid.

I grabbed her arm outside the classroom and shoved her.

"I trusted you," I remember screaming. "I thought you were different, but you're worse than everyone else because you know me and you're trying to steal my life."

She stared at me.

"Antonella," she said slowly, "have you ever asked me anything about my life?"

She proceeded to tell me about her problems, her anorexia, her abusive mom, the fact that she'd moved out and supported herself since she was seventeen.

I cut her off. "I don't care," I told her. "I don't have time to listen to anything you're saying, and I don't believe you anyway."

She DM'ed me a long, rambling message that night, about how she was sorry she hurt my feelings, but she had her own issues, and I read it, but I told her I didn't.

"You're a pathetic liar, and you're boring too. You're just another privileged Jewish girl whose greatest asset is her trust fund."

"I'm an immigrant, I don't have a trust fund (I wish)" She wrote back. "Do me one favour, keep us Jews and whatever trauma porn you're into out of your mouth, or you'll be in trouble."

I was a little rattled by that one, I admit, but then my brother, who was a cop, pointed out that the last part sounded like a threat. He got one of his buddies to call her like she was in trouble.

I heard she was so scared, asking about a permanent record, like she was in high school, almost crying.

I found another girl in class who also hated her, and we laughed about her. I even found two of her exes, one on social media, one in real life, and we laughed at what a loser she was. At least one of them made sure the conversation even got back to her.

I honestly never felt bad about the way I treated her. When you play with fire you get burned, and I'm a motherfucking forest fire.

She blocked me everywhere, but I follow her career. Her success infuriates me when I let it; I should have burned her up, killed any urge for her to create or even exist, but there she is, becoming famous and respected even as I struggle.

Once, in the last few years I actually missed her. We have a mutual friend, and Milquetoast refused to say anything bad about me. I don't know if it was fear, or awe like before, if my friend was right and she just didn't care anymore or if she was just trying to take the high road, but in that moment, just for a moment, I missed her.

Luckily, I let it pass.

All Good Things Take Time

MIRIAM WAS LYING in her bed in her messy apartment, her legs stretched over her faded white and yellow polka dot sheets. Adam was writing his last exam. He'd been keeping more of his stuff at her apartment, in preparation for three weeks later, when they'd be living together. Dread tiptoed like a family of ants marching through her stomach, revealing her fears one by one. Rent was much higher in New York than it was in Toronto. They'd only been able to afford a tiny one bedroom, so she knew she was going to have to give away a good chunk of her stuff, guitars and keyboards, art books and notepads, and for potentially twenty-four hours a day, Adam would be around. There'd be no mystery left.

Miriam reached for the glass of lukewarm spearmint tea on her bedside table. Her throat was on fire. Every sip felt like she'd swallowed a lit match. It reminded her of having strep when she was a kid. She always wanted to be sick enough to not have to go to school.

Her mother would come into her room at 7:30 am, on her way to her job as an occupational therapist in Tel Aviv. Her mom worked exclusively with children with physical challenges. Sometimes they were born with them, like Shelley, a brilliant girl who spoke four languages and had spina bifida. Others like Nitzan were in a wheelchair after being in a car accident. Her mom was always telling Miriam how lucky she was to be healthy. It drove her crazy. Her dad was a doctor who looked straight past whatever was wrong with her. He looked through her, which everyone said was because she looked like his sister Estee, who had died when they were young.

Whenever she was sick, her mom would lay a cool palm on her forehead, and leave mint tea with leaves cut fresh from a plant on their kitchen window sill. She'd also leave her a pill to bring down her fever.

When sister Hadas got chicken pox, she rolled around in her sheets, snuck bites of her food and even rubbed her used tissues on her nose and eyes. She traced the crater deep scar on her left cheek, a remnant of aggressive chicken pox scratching. All the oatmeal baths and calamine lotion hadn't helped. Her mom had looked at her with an intensity she usually saved for her work, or the kind of tearjerker movies she watched with her aunts when her dad was away for a conference.

"Miri," she'd said softly. "You're so beautiful. We can fix this."

She went upstairs into her bathroom and brought her a jar of her expensive vitamin E cream. She sat in her mother's lap like she was four, instead of almost twelve, and closed her eyes as her mom softly dabbed it on her.

"You have to use your ring finger, see this one here, when you put cream on your face. It's gentler."

Miriam nodded dreamily. She felt so loved. When her mom got up to get dinner ready, she went to the bathroom and washed it off. None of her sisters had scars.

It was strange that her throat hurt. She'd had her tonsils taken out when she was ten.

Her mother had gone with her the day before her surgery to buy all of her favourite soft foods, ice cream, Jell-O, and she had made *Shmeed*, Moroccan semolina soup, with cilantro and turmeric.

She'd wanted to be a famous surgeon. As a kid, she pored over her dad's old medical textbooks. Science was her favourite subject, until she got to high school, and it was clear that she'd never be able to keep up with the nerdy geniuses in her classes. It was no surprise to anyone who knew her that she'd gotten engaged to a future doctor. If they seemed like an odd pairing to some, Adam would tell people that they were equally driven in their careers, he with medicine, she with her music. In fact, he'd sometimes add, his end game was neurology, and everyone knew that music could alter brain structure and function.

She played her last show in Toronto the night before they left. It was a small club on Queen St. W., but the place was packed. Her band was great, and every song swelled and stretched across the room. By the end, when she sang her last original song, "I Can't Believe (I'm Leaving You)" both she and the audience were crying. Her electric blue mascara streaked cobalt tears down her cheeks. She sang a cover of the PJ Harvey song "A Place Called Home," and looked over at Adam, standing near the side of the stage. She'd never seen him teary eyed before.

When they finally got to New York, their apartment in Brooklyn, which he'd chosen, was like she'd imagined.

She could only sleep if it was really dark, and their apartment was never quite dark enough. Light from the neighbour's porch, the red and blue neon Bar London sign from across the street, even the faint early morning sun, always managed to break through.

Adam rolled onto his side, his coppery eyebrows knitting together like a welcome mat.

"You're going to suffocate."

She buried her face.

Lately all of her habits seemed to annoy him. He complained about the way she slept, the way she chain-smoked on the balcony, the way she'd lie in the hottest bath her body could take, using all their hot water, and sometimes falling asleep in it. She'd step out of the bathroom wrapped in towels, her legs heavy and her eyes glazed.

Every morning, at around 5 am, she could hear a faint scratching. She got up one day to see what it was. On the floor near the fridge was the smooth, golden caramel of a medjool date. It had long feelers and legs that were covered in bumps. It was twice the size of the ones she'd seen growing up in Israel. North America was supposed to be cleaner. She poked its hard shell tentatively with her slipper. It flew a few feet in the air, then scuttled under the fridge.

"Adam," she yelled, "we have cockroaches."

Adam sat up. He had creases on his cheek from sleeping on his side.

She padded into the bedroom and sat down next to him on his side of the bed.

"Yup," he murmured. "I saw one near the toilet last night. I looked online. They thrive on water."

"They're disgusting. They're worse than the ones we have in Israel."

He didn't respond.

Miriam decided to try a different tack. "Don't they spread diseases?"

He sighed. "I think so, but babe, this is New York. I saw a whole bunch of red ones piled up next to each other near the subway grate yesterday and took a photo. Everyone has them. I don't think there's much we can do."

Her lip curled in disgust. "We could stop cooking and eating in here. We could tie up our garbage."

He reached for her hand. "Yeah, we could be cleaner. But we live in a building." She looked away. "I'll call the super in an hour or two, and see what he says. Maybe he can call us an exterminator. In the meantime, come back to bed."

She flopped down beside him, defeated.

Adam had started university just a few weeks after they arrived. Miriam had taken the first job she'd found, as an assistant at a dog grooming parlour. She'd spent her mornings brushing dogs' fur, and holding them as her boss, Jacqueline, a warm but brittle looking woman, cut or sheared their hair. Jacqueline always spoke to the dogs like they were people.

"And how is Miss Georgie doing this morning?" she'd ask an arthritic Golden Doodle. "Sammy is always crotchety until we walk him, aren't you?" she asked a soft eared Spaniel mix, and Miriam would wait, patiently, for the dog to tip its head to the side, like it was listening, or bark or growl some kind of response. Some of the puppies, including a beagle mix named Chiquita, would leap into her arms whenever she went up to them. She had to walk the dogs twice a day, and she did it with headphones on, listening to music, and ignoring the blaring traffic as she gathered her thoughts, and got song ideas. One day, a woman brought in a ginger Pomeranian named Lyric. She was a crotchety older dog, who looked like a baby fox, but it turned out she was owned by a music publisher named Janet Stone. Miriam charmed Janet into listening to YouTube clips and recordings of her music, and Janet liked them.

"You write great pop hooks," Janet said. "These songs could be all over the radio." Miriam was excited until Janet explained that she wanted to sign her to a publishing deal, to write music for other artists. She could make money, and connections, Janet explained, by being part of a team who wrote pop music for young artists on major labels.

Miriam didn't really want to entertain it. "I want to be the star," she blurted out, before she could stop herself. "I want to write music for myself."

Janet looked her up and down. "You're too old for pop," she said and poked the side of Miriam's face with a long nail. "You're pretty, but you look too close to twenty-five. There's a lot more money in writing and producing. Trust me, I'm doing you a favour."

Miriam was crushed at first, but she decided to take the opportunity. Her first meeting was in a record label's boardroom. She had to try, with the help of two older men and a much older woman, to craft sexually suggestive but not explicit lyrics, for a fifteen-year-old singer whom the label was trying to break. Bella was tiny and pretty, with long blond hair, a big white smile and golden skin. She was moderately talented, with a bouncy personality and a huge online following. The male producers and writers would buy her lunch, or coffee, tease her then offer to spend extra time working with her. Bella's mom, her manager, would spray her with perfume, fluff up her hair, and push her to the studio door. Sometimes Miriam and the writers would argue about the right lyrics for hours. Still, the money was good. If Miriam agreed to get songwriting credit, and split royalties with the other writers, the money would be great, but she'd have to wait a long time to get it. If she took money upfront, her name wouldn't be on the song, but she'd make serious cash. Once, they gave her four thousand dollars. Plus, the musicians knew how to have a good time. One night, to celebrate one of their singers signing a major label deal, they invited her to the record exec's fancy Brooklyn brownstone for a tea party. Instead of cucumber sandwiches, every guest was served a several grams of soft, crumbly cocaine that was spooned, like powdered sugar on a crepe, onto their dainty porcelain tea plates from a fancy silver tray in the middle of the table. As a party gift, everyone got to keep their tiny silver serving spoon.

After that party, Miriam quit her job at the dog parlour, and made a deal with Janet that she would write songs for them two days a week, and use their studios to record her own music once a week. She spent her evenings and days off wandering through Brooklyn and Williamsburg, with headphones on, combing through bookstores and record stores, listening and browsing and occasionally buying, and seeing bands play. Everyone she met in New York was talented. She met actors and musicians, writers for TV and stage, critics, essay writers, and novelists, and they all wore their creativity and style casually, as if the ideas in themselves were not enough somehow. They were so self-effacing. Miriam had never really felt that she had as much to prove. To be successful in pop, she reasoned, you didn't need to be the best, or the most innovative. You just needed to work hard and be really charming. She was always confident that she could win people over.

She met musicians who invited her to join them for coffee, or drinks, or occasionally onstage or in the studio. There was one guy, Sebastian, with intense eyes, long dark hair, and a half smirk. He eyed her the way a cat gazes at a perfectly shiny, slow-moving goldfish. She had to admit, it felt good. There were women too; Carolyn, a make-up artist with a face like a Madame Alexander doll, and a body like a burlesque dancer from the 1940's, and Margalit, an Israeli pastry chef who was wry, and sometimes spoke Hebrew with a heavy Brooklyn accent.

She assumed that Adam knew, though they never spoke about it. He knew she'd never been monogamous before. As long as it wasn't in his face, she reasoned, there was no way he could be humiliated.

She went out or wrote or recorded most nights while he stayed home and studied. She went to a drop in poetry class one night at the 92 Y in the city. She met two sisters, Cleo and Stacey, who were actors. Cleo had recently landed a spot in a national Ford Minivan commercial, and had a YouTube channel called *Dear Cleo* with more than twenty thousand subscribers. Stacey had a part in an off Broadway play. They convinced her that an acting class would be great for her stage presence, and she signed up for Acting for Amateurs one night at the Barrow Group. Miriam often invited Adam to come with her, to parties, to bars, to see shows, but he'd shake his head and promise to try to meet her later. She'd find him asleep at his boxy Ikea desk, or sprawled out across the middle of their bed so she couldn't get into with him. It always disappointed her that he never stayed up worrying about her. She left cups of half finished green tea all over the apartment. She was getting into reading tea leaves, she told him. She always wanted to read his, but he wouldn't let her. He was getting annoyed about all the money she was spending.

"You have to spend money to make money," she said, as she tried to explain away new headshots, expensive studio time, the expanding of piles of sexy stage clothes and bright, glittery make up. She had twenty thousand dollars worth of credit card debt.

Miriam was always frustrated that he didn't care enough to argue with her.

"I want more passion," she said one night, when he bought her a bunch of white lilies.

She thought about the way Sebastian had tossed her across his bed, taking her from behind. He picked her up with one arm, like she was made of paper. It felt like the deepest state of oblivion.

She walked up to him and whispered in his ear: "I want it a little more rough" but when he tried it later, it just felt like bad acting.

Adam took her to a bar in their neighbourhood that also had a venue for live music. "Let's see if can get you a regular gig here," he said, over Mediterranean tapas served with homebrewed hibiscus kombucha. She rolled her eyes, and her press on eyelashes started to peel off.

"I'm sick of all this hipster shit," she said quietly. "I want to be a legitimate mainstream singer."

"You will be," he said flatly. "All good things take time."

As soon as they got home, she was on him about the cockroaches again.

He pulled out his phone. "Apparently we have to buy Roach Away. See this? It tells you how."

"I have to take a shower. Can you pick some up after work? I can help you set it up when I get back."

Miriam started researching online. Some websites mentioned gel baits, others talked about boric acid. She was supposed to buy boric acid and sprinkle it in a fine layer, like a snow drift. One website told her to mix it with confectioner's sugar. Another one told her she could buy boric acid in capsules. Some women, it said, used it to treat yeast infections.

The next day, she spent an hour in the hardware store a few blocks away, then stopped in at the health food store on the next block. She spent forty-five minutes in Walmart in Flatbush. She came home and measured the boric acid and sugar carefully with a measuring cup. I must look so domestic, she thought, like a house wife baking a cake. She started laughing. The boric acid and sugar mix looked chalky. She stuck her finger in it and licked it. She took a handful, mixed it in with a glass of water, and drank. She looked in her Walmart bag. She'd bought a Duncan Hines cake mix that she wanted to make now. She mixed it in a bowl and turned the oven on. She took out the stronger stuff, the Roach Away and spread it in the other corners of the kitchen. She licked her fingers again before she washed her hands.

An hour later, she called Adam. "I don't feel so well," she said. "I'm really nauseous and woozy. I have this bright red rash all over my arms and hands. It's really itchy and painful, and it came out of nowhere."

When Adam came home he found her lying on the kitchen floor in a pool of green and blue vomit.

"Babe," he screamed. "Are you okay?"

Miriam looked up at him groggily. "I don't know."

They rushed her to Maimonides Medical Centre. She had a fever. They took her temperature, her pulse and her blood pressure. She explained that she'd been baking a cake, that they'd had roaches, so she went out and bought what the nice man at Walmart had most highly recommended.

The exhausted looking doctor, with a black mustache and thin smile and his friendly, heavy-set nurse were gentle.

They put a tube through her mouth into her stomach to wash out the poison. They gave her an IV of fluids.

"Is it possible," the doctor asked her, "that you accidentally ingested some of the boric acid?"

Miriam's eyes widened. "I don't know," she said. "I guess I've been a little stressed."

Adam leaned over and reached for her hand.

As a final precaution, they put a camera down her throat to see how badly she'd burned her esophagus and stomach. The doctor explained the dangers of boric acid poisoning.

"People have died," he said. "You were really lucky, but you have to be more careful."

* * *

The next weekend, they were invited to relatives of Adam's who lived in Midwood. They sat at their Shabbat table, and Miriam felt comforted by the familiar ritual. The family was Ashkenazi, so the food was amusingly different, cold slices of gefilte fish with a carrot, chicken soup and surprisingly tasty cholent, without the cinnamon and chickpeas of her mom's, and the atmosphere was more subdued, and quieter, but it was still a relief to instantly feel like she belonged. It had been months since she and Adam had kept Shabbat. Adam was culturally Jewish, but he was not religious.

Her stomach was still swollen and bloated, and when his aunt Barbara pulled her aside in the kitchen, to quietly congratulate her, she played along. She laughed and touched her stomach tenderly. She put a finger to her lips. "Shhh," she said, "and thank you."

Miriam poked at her stomach gingerly. Convincing everyone that she was pregnant had been surprisingly easy.

She drank more Perrier and Coke so that her stomach looked bloated. She ate every decadent thing she convinced herself she could never otherwise have—four cheese ravioli in cream sauce, thin crust pizza with mushroom and truffle oil, thick, sweet strawberry milkshakes from the twenty-four-hour diner across the street from their apartment. Adam would come home at night and find her digging into Nutella straight from the jar, or tearing into a bag of his salt and vinegar potato chips with feverish glee. He'd always gotten on her case before about how strict her diet was, and he told her how relieved he was to see her enjoying food.

She put on twelve pounds alarmingly quickly. Luckily, she gained weight in her breasts and in her stomach. The weight put extra pressure on her diaphragm, and she found that she could actually hit lower notes better. Adam opened doors for her, and offered her his chair, so she finally gave herself permission to be less frantic about writing and recording songs. She spent hours reading articles and online forums about pregnancy. She was always careful. Every month she inserted soft, square sponges that her friend, Marcy, an adult film star from Queens whose stage name was Paris Diamond, gave her so that Adam would never see her using tampons. Whenever he ate tuna or salmon, she'd make a face and say she had to leave the room. When the building got brand new rubber mats at its front door, she complained that the smell made her nauseous.

Adam had looked terrified when she'd first told him, his mouth cartoon zig zag of incredulity and dread but he quickly came around. They were at his favourite bar in Williamsburg when she told him. He had just ordered their usual drinks. His was called an Ai Wei Wei. Hers was a Green Baby. It was made of vodka, matcha, and pineapple.

A band called The Turquoise Squids was playing. The singer was wearing a tank top and a floral knee length skirt. Everything about her was languid, her voice, the way she swayed, not making eye contact with the crowd. She found her effortlessness obnoxious. Miriam was wearing a long oversized Nas Illmatic T-shirt with the sleeves cut off as a dress. Her heavy gold metal hoop earrings were starting to give her a headache. She had recently cut her hair into a sharp, slightly uneven short style. She wanted to look like Edie Sedgewick in *Ciao Manhattan*. Adam thought she looked like a five-year-old playing hairdresser. "You're lucky you're so pretty, Miri," he said, and gave her a kiss on her forehead. She leaned in across the table, pushed her drink away, looked him in the eye and said, "I'm pregnant." She'd reached into her purse and pulled out a positive pregnancy test. She'd asked around, and it turned out Cleo and Stacey had a cousin who'd recently gotten pregnant. Stacey pocketed one of her tests, put it in a Ziploc bag and sanitized her hands. Miriam paid her two hundred dollars. She knew Adam would want proof. "I can't believe it," he kept saying. The next week, she paid Cleo to call pretending to be the receptionist at a walk in clinic to confirm their results. It had now sunk in, and he hugged her.

Miriam knew she could only keep this up for so long. They'd have to tell their families, and people would expect her to look like someone carrying a growing child soon. She started to sweat. She was going to have to have a miscarriage. On the one hand, it was a relief, but it made her sad because she was growing attached to the idea of being pregnant. Pregnant women had always seemed so beautiful, with their longer, thicker hair and glowing skin. One of her cousins had flaming trails of acne all over her cheeks and forehead, and another threw up every single day for nine months, and had to go on IV drips, but in the end, they both had an adorable, brand new human who loved them more than anything.

Miriam had read that miscarriages often happened in the first trimester, for reasons that were beyond anyone's understanding. She told the writers she was going to the hospital. She held her stomach and told Janet that she was in a lot of pain.

She remembered what her father had told her. "When someone shows up at an emergency room with a low blood count, doctors take notice and order a CBC, a complete blood count test, right away. If a person has a severe infection, their white or red cells would be down, which would alert doctors to the problem."

It would be painful, Miriam knew, to a cut to an artery, but some quick swipes of her Swiss Army knife to her legs or arms would do it. She just wanted to get it over with. She looked down at her lap. She was going to have to bleed down there too, if she was going to convince anyone.

She had researched everything online, from self-induced abortions, to ending nonexistent pregnancies like hers, and she'd found that women often used kitchen utensils to make themselves bleed. Knives produced lacerations that were so obvious a doctor might be able to put it together. On account of the roaches, they had nearly nothing in their kitchen. She took a cab to a Target not far from the studio. She perused the kitchen wares carefully and finally settled on a small metal lemon zester. She also bought a pack of extra strength aspirin and a bottle of water. She ducked into the bathroom at the Target. She took off her white skirt and underwear. She took four aspirins first, and then opened the zester. She rubbed her vulva with such force that she pulled skin off. She poked herself carefully after and it bled to the touch. She quickly dabbed the spot with a cotton pad and a small jar full of salt water, honey and chamomile that she kept in her purse. It was a brilliant home remedy that her grandmother used on her and her sisters as kids to treat their cuts. It would make the cuts seem less noticeable.

She put her underwear and skirt back on. She took one more aspirin just for good measure. She wrapped the lemon zester and the box of aspirins in toilet paper and threw them in the tampon box. It was starting to hurt. She was starting to have cramps. She edged herself carefully back into the brightly lit entrance of the store. She was feeling faint.

"Help," she yelled, and made eye contact with the nearest cashier. "I'm pregnant and I can't stop bleeding."

She felt dizzy. She looked down. Driblets of blood, like fuchsia dewdrops and pearls, formed beneath her.

"Someone call 911," someone yelled. Miriam crashed down heavily on the linoleum floor.

"Don't worry," a twenty-something paramedic in navy blue said, running up to her. "There's a hospital close to here. We'll take care of you."

It was exciting to see young, attractive paramedics look panicked.

"I have heavy vaginal bleeding," she said, "heavier than my heaviest flow." She paused and looked up at their navy uniforms. "I'm almost eleven weeks pregnant."

She caught the look that passed between them of barely concealed panic.

"I'm going to need you not to move," one of them said. "We're going to put you on a stretcher and take you to New York Presbyterian." They lifted her carefully and carried her out of the store and into the parking lot. She felt like an ancient Greek queen being carried through a crowd. One of her favourite accessories when she performed was a gold leaf flower wreath that she wished she was wearing it right now. All that was missing was someone to stand there, fanning her with palm leaves.

Miriam was seen very quickly when she got to the hospital. A nurse wheeled into an ultrasound room and shook her head as she helped her onto the examination table. She closed the door so that Miriam could get undressed. Miriam reached into her purse and dabbed herself one more time with her grandmother's solution. A grandfatherly doctor came in and gave her a pelvic exam. He had heavy but experienced hands.

"I see you have some spotting," Dr. Schultz said, and Miriam nodded.

"Your cervix is dilated," he said, and she sighed with relief.

She winced at his touch, and he kept apologizing. "I'm sorry, but it's important to be thorough," he said. "You might need what we call a D&C, a dilation and curettage. It's a brief surgical procedure where we dilate the cervix and use a special instrument to scrape the uterine lining to remove any tissue that could cause an infection."

Miriam had read about this, of course. She was slightly disappointed when he said she didn't need one.

"Up to twenty-five percent of pregnancies end in miscarriage in the first thirteen weeks," he said. "Was this your first pregnancy?"

Miriam nodded, real tears welling up in her eyes.

"I'd been having really bad back pain for the last couple of days, but I didn't think it was connected." She paused. "Maybe it's my fault. Maybe I should have come in sooner."

The doctor shook his head. “It’s not your fault. It might not have helped even if you had come in sooner.” He looked at her, his eyes brimming with sympathy. “I have some brochures that will help to explain these things. In the meantime, is there someone who can come and pick you up?”

She bit the inside of her lip. “My husband.”

When he arrived forty-five minutes later, Adam’s face was the colour of the blanched almonds Miriam’s mom used to make Moroccan marzipan. She was surprised by how much pain she was still in. She was too weak from the blood loss to be as angry with him as she wanted to be for not getting there sooner.

The whole thing made Miriam really wanting to get pregnant. Once a month had passed, they had the wildest, freest sex they’d ever had, in their bed, on their balcony, on the subway late at night when no one was watching them. At his insistence, Adam came with her to get her hormone levels checked. They went to an obstetrician he found when she was eight weeks along. She had the ultrasound, waited to go into the claustrophobic, closet sized room, where she had to lie down and have cold jelly squirted onto her small but growing stomach. Adam squeezed her hand and begged the young technician to confirm what he already knew but desperately needed to hear: everything was normal. Everything was developing as it should be.

It was clear that he worried about her in a way that he never had before. He got her an Uber account when she told them that the muggy, sweaty smells in the subway made her gag. He texted her during the day. He came home as soon as his classes were over. They never talked about the miscarriage. It would cause her too much anxiety to even think about it, she told him.

He nodded. "It's all behind us now," he said.

"You never know," she said, "but I really hope so."

If You're Not Careful, You'll be Lonely

ARNIE LISTED HIS AGE as twenty-eight on the app, and his photos were arty, all dark colours against his green eyes and pale skin, and sharp angles against his cheekbones and slim frame. What Sadie had gotten, when she bothered to actually open it lately, were either dick pics or too much information about a person she might never actually meet. Everything about Arnie was interesting but vague. He had one of those jobs, like graphic design or IT, she couldn't remember which, and his messages were short, but smart.

When Sadie saw him in real life, it was immediately clear that he'd lied about his age. In the dim lighting on the corner of Grace Street in Little Italy where they stood facing each other, she found herself looking him up and down. He wore a navy wool coat, grey beanie, copper blonde hair a little too light, like it was on its way to grey. He smiled at her, and the crow's feet that crisscrossed the corners of his eyes flashed. She reached out, instinctively, before she could stop herself, and stroked the side of his face. The beginnings of stubble pricked the tips of her fingers and felt like tiny bolts of electricity.

Sadie was surprised that she didn't feel angry or deceived, but merely curious about why he'd withheld his age. She preferred older men and silently guessed him to be about forty. She reached for his hand.

Originally, when they emailed, they couldn't decide where to go, so they'd arranged to meet in front of a restaurant that served slightly undercooked pasta dishes in Pomodoro or Alfredo sauce for less than ten dollars a plate, a restaurant whose walls were decorated with yellowing thick Sharpie signed black and white photos of minor celebrities from the eighties.

It was nine o clock, and she'd already had dinner. She avoided eating in public whenever possible. She didn't trust restaurants, even what other people insisted were the healthy kind. The obvious things like fried food, sugar, red meat, dairy and carbs were obviously off limits. She tried not to have fruit because of their high sugar content, but occasionally allowed herself to indulge in an apple, or a banana. She ate a variation on the same thing every day: salad with dressing on the side, a sugar-free zero-fat strawberry yoghurt, six raw almonds, vegetable stir fries with lean protein like tofu or chicken breasts, and a small bowl of bean soup, or egg whites. She didn't live to eat, she ate to live a long life. Her hard-partying, coke-drinking and barbeque chips for breakfast eating brother Jeff drove drunk when she was sixteen and died a few days later. He was nineteen. She decided then that she wasn't going to be anything like him.

She went to the gym seven days a week because she was an athlete. She used to like dating body builders with fitness regimes more stringent than her own. Watching them eat a dozen raw eggs, or watching their blenders whirl with protein powders, Creatine, and Anabolic Steroids was like foreplay. She liked that they could lift her high off the ground with one arm, twirl her like a paper ballerina with just one or two fingers. They made her feel weightless. She liked that they understood her need to weigh her chicken, to log even her sugar free gum in her tracking apps. Most of all, she liked that they understood when she said that the gym was the place that she felt most free to be herself. She'd run and dance on the treadmill, cheesy pop pouring out of her headphones, laughing her loudest laugh at the antics of the Kardashians on the flat screen in front of her. When she hit her stride, usually about twenty minutes into her two-hour workouts, when the endorphins first hit her bloodstream, it felt like she was flying. She felt invincible and giddy.

The longest relationship she'd ever had was Bruno. She met him at an elite gym she had to give up after their breakup. After their first few heady months together, she texted a friend who'd moved to another city to say that she couldn't believe that someone she loved, loved her too. He took her to Vienna and Munich. She had holidays with his family, his mother even bought her a Swarovski crystal necklace one year. They never pressed about her family or why she didn't talk to them. If you'd ask her in that first year, if she ever thought she'd cheat on him, she would have been outraged. But after almost four years together, when they still weren't living together, she'd heard all of his stories at least five times, and their sex life having dwindled to practically nothing, she did. It was another body builder, of course, and they were discreet at first, until they weren't. When he found out, Bruno was furious, and refused to ever speak to her again.

When she was nineteen, her mother took her out for dinner, and over drinks explained that there were different kinds of men. There were the kind that you married, the ones with good livelihoods that came from good families—and then there were lovers. Lovers, she explained, were what sustained her and Sadie's father's relationship. Sadie had known that her parents situation was weird, that her dad often slept in the basement, and occasionally didn't come home, but she'd never asked how or why they'd stayed together.

Arnie didn't look like the kind of guy who worked out, but he also didn't look like the kind who loved to eat.

It was her idea for their date to be a walk, but he agreed enthusiastically.

In one of his messages, he told her he loved her full lips and round blue eyes. *Sadie means princess, doesn't it?* he wrote. *This is going to sound like a line, but it isn't—you look like a real life Disney Princess.*

She thought about all the work that went into it, all the facials and fillers and make up, the contouring and Face Tuning.

She loved Disney, but didn't answer, not even to say thank you. That night he told her she looked like Tinkerbell. He said he liked her tiny hands.

She thought of the palm reader she saw after she graduated from her MBA program who had pointed out the prominence and depth of a line that criss-crossed through the centre of the triangle shape on her left hand. *You'll be very successful in your career*, she told her. *But if you're not careful you'll be very lonely.*

Sadie had gotten a job in marketing almost right out of school and was climbing the ranks. She'd almost laughed because she was always lonely, whether she had friends or a relationship, or she was on her own.

She'd stopped talking to two of her close friends when they'd told her they were worried about her eating, and the way she buried herself in work. Claire she'd known since high school, Ella since her undergrad. She told them that, if they didn't stop being so judgemental, she'd have to stop being friends with both of them. And they didn't, so she did. She thought of them as creamy Oreo ice cream and crispy, salty French fries, treasured childhood treats that no longer had a place in her adult life.

She knew that they were jealous of her. When they said they worried about her hooking up with random guys, she knew that they secretly wanted more exciting lives. She had total freedom, while they had to be thankful that anyone would want them. Ella had recently gotten engaged, and Claire was living with a guy who'd never worked a day in his life. They wanted to have kids, but what's pregnancy when you already have a jelly belly? She'd worked so hard especially lately, to look more streamlined. She didn't want to lose her abs, all that hard earned muscle. She didn't want stretch marks and cellulite. She didn't want to remove her nipple rings and her clit ring. She didn't want her vagina to get permanently stretched out like a rubber band. She couldn't be friends with people whose values she couldn't respect. She should have done it years before. It wasn't hard at all.

* * *

Arnie took her to a park and kissed her. His touch was gentle, like he was trying too hard to win her over. It didn't matter, really, orgasms turned the nagging criticisms in her brain into blissful, crackling static. For a few hours she didn't have to think or worry. Now all she had to do was relax enough to get there. She took his hand and guided it to her thigh, slid his index finger underneath the soft folds of her skirt. Soon he was grinning, thin fingers grazing the waistband of her underwear. She was smiling, relaxing. They took an Uber back to his apartment. It was a studio, tiny, with a gold statue of Buddha and a large, king sized bed with dark sheets. He had a framed poster of Lil Wayne—she wasn't sure was if it was ironic or sincere—and a calico cat named Camille.

He unbuttoned her shirt gingerly and stared at her while she lay in his bed, biting her bottom lip. He kissed her neck, kissed her collarbones, licked her hardening nipples.

When he texted her two days later she agreed to see him again. This time he insisted on taking her to a restaurant. *It's called Noche Oscura,* he said, *which means dark night in Spanish. You choose what you want and then you get taken to a pitch black room, where all your food is brought to you. If you need the bathroom, you have to call for a waiter to guide you. It's amazing, you'll see.*

They met at the entrance of the restaurant. They were both wearing dark jeans and black leather jackets. He pointed it out and laughed. He told her how beautiful she looked in her flouncy silk shirt, with the corset top, told her how sexy her high heels were, and held open the door for her.

He ordered a hundred-dollar bottle of French wine for them, while they waited in the cavernous bowels of the bar area. She surprised herself by accepting a glass happily, and downing it quickly, without even being certain of the calorie math.

She asked him about his romantic past. Had he been in love? How long was his longest relationship?

She was older than the women he usually dated. His last girlfriend was twenty. It had been fun, he said, but he'd gotten bored.

He reached for her knee under the table and gripped it softly with his fingertips.

He'd been in exactly one serious relationship with a woman his own age. It had lasted for five years. They'd owned a house in the suburbs and had an Italian Greyhound. He didn't think he'd ever want that again, but here she was—a vision who'd made him reconsider.

She wasn't sure if she wanted him, but it was nice to know that he wanted her. A waitress took their orders and led them to a table in the dark. She downed two more glasses of wine within half an hour. Soon she was giggling, her voice sounding like a deranged squeak, and she could hear herself, but she couldn't stop the words and feelings from coming out. She started talking about her past, about Bruno. *I am terrified right now, terrified of you. You have this great smile, and you're classy, this restaurant is expensive and my former friends would kill to be here—and I'm scared. I'm scared because I usually fuck things up.*

He was silent which spurred her on. She'd seemed so different the first time, so completely together, so guarded, and now, just a little wine and a second date, and she was bursting at the seams, like a carefully wrapped present shedding its ribbons and its paper only to reveal something cracked and probably defective underneath. He knew she sensed it, saw him looking at her oddly, but she couldn't stop herself, not now, not when she still had so much she had to tell him.

She found herself asking him again if he'd ever been in love, you know, really been in love, like when you feel like you could die for someone if they asked you to, when someone is truly the centre of your world.

He shook his head. *You know, I'm not sure I have,* he murmured, and she paused for a second, took a quick breath and then continued.

The first time I was in high school, she said. *He was a lot more popular than me and I liked him for two years before he asked me out. We watched movies and football games together, and it was perfect until he pressured me into giving him a blowjob. He bugged me for weeks, and when I finally did it, he dumped me the next day. I was so depressed and nothing helped.*

The only thing that helped me was fantasizing about Zayn Malik. He was still in One Direction back then. I knew everything about him, that he had hazel eyes, that his favourite color was red, that his family was from Bradford in Northern England, that his dad was from Pakistan, that his favourite food was chicken and his favourite song of all was "Thriller" by Michael Jackson. I thought we were perfect for each other. I even looked into converting to Islam.

He felt his body inching back a little.

Lots of people have celebrity crushes, he said.

I treated Zayn like an imaginary boyfriend. It's not like I was five, with imaginary friends. I knew it was weird, but once I started I couldn't stop. I talked about him like I knew him. I even imagined marrying him. I spent hours on the internet looking at wedding dresses I'd buy, you know, because the sky was the limit with his kind of money. I looked up Muslim weddings and their after parties, so colourful and full of the kind of tradition and culture that my family doesn't have. I imagined how he'd ask me, how I'd say yes. I imagined the fifty-thousand-dollar diamond he would buy me—because I was sure I was worth a fortune. She laughed mirthlessly.

I imagined him finally giving in, letting me have the exotic beach wedding I'd always wanted in Maui or Fiji. I made wedding invitations. I bought this expensive tissue paper to print them on, got my cousin who was a graphic designer to make them incredibly beautiful, with lacy script and gold designs. I told her it was for a school project. Somehow one got passed to my ex, who told everyone I'd lost my mind, but to my face he said he was happy for me. At least he assumed I was over him.

Arnie sighed. He wasn't sure how much more he wanted to know. He wondered if she'd actually stalked him, if she'd met him and ripped a hair from his head, or got herself arrested hiding in his bushes.

She reached her hand across the table. *Don't worry. I'm over him now. I have one tattoo*—she pointed to her left rib—*that means Be True To Who You Are in Arabic, like a tiny version of his. But I don't even listen to his or their music anymore. I never met him and I don't really want to. I don't know if anything could ever match the fantasy I had.*

He paid for their meal, which came to roughly two hundred and sixty dollars, and he tried not to grimace, though he was pretty sure she'd be too drunk to notice.

He called them an Uber, which he paid for too. In the darkness of the backseat, he pawed at her a little. He bit her collarbones and played with the pendant she was wearing around her neck, before giving her nipples a tweak.

She said she liked his apartment as they walked in.

He said, *I have everything I want right here, everything I'll never need or want in the world*. He added, *I'm sure most women wouldn't want to hear that.*

She shrugged. *I'm not most women*, she said, and grinned. *I just want to have a good time.*

He laughed. He wondered if her bedroom wall was covered in Zayn Malik posters. At least this part of the night wouldn't disappoint.

He grabbed her shoulders, looked her in the eye to see if she meant it or not, but her eyes were murky and swimming with alcohol and he couldn't tell.

He grabbed the silk scarf that she was wearing around her neck and used it to tie her hands up. She grinned and let him go down on her, let him touch her and lick her everywhere, let him enter her without a condom on, let him come inside her. She moaned as she felt it trickle down, so warm, onto her thighs. He untied her, and they cuddled for the requisite fifteen minutes before falling asleep.

She woke up at 8:30 the next morning. He was lying next to her, out cold. She crept out of bed, and into his tiny bathroom. She found her underwear and clothes on his floor and got dressed. She thought of the costs of the previous night: the drinks, the food, the cab. She probably should have offered to contribute. She found a scrap of paper and wrote him a note that she rewrote three times before settling on: *Thanks for a fun night*, S.

She opened her wallet. She had four hundred dollars in cash but she needed forty for the morning after pill. She took out a hundred, plus three twenty dollars bills and placed them on his nightstand.

She erased his number from her phone. She couldn't quite remember what she'd said but somehow she knew she'd given too much away, and since she didn't quite know what, she knew she couldn't risk talking to him again. Luckily, he never called.

Smoke Show

ANGELICA WAS ON HER WAY to the party when Mateo called her a smoke show, which annoyed her because even though she knew it was a compliment, it hardly felt like one. It made her think of smoke and mirrors, like she was hiding something that could fundamentally change his opinion of her. It was a feeling she was used to, a feeling that she'd been living with for years. It was disarming, like if a teenager broke into a science lab and accidentally discovered a brand-new law of physics.

They met for the first time in an expensive, white sculptural looking parking lot a few metres from a candy-coloured graffiti wall in Wynwood. It was off camera, which the producers were dead set against. But you only got one first impression, and she wanted to see what he really thought of her.

For a lot of the women, Mateo was perfect, soft Golden Retriever brown eyes, thick caramel coloured hair, a sweet, endless stream of flirting and compliments, which when delivered by him somehow sounded sincere. There was the small gold crucifix around his neck, peaking out of the downy chest hair from his one unbuttoned button. There was the fact that he was born in Hialeah, still spoke Spanish, and was close to his family, but had made enough money to own a yacht, a few small boats, and a big house in Coconut Grove. There was both Dom and Cristal, bunches of roses in pastel Jordan almond colours, one on one dates where the women competed against each other like this was their one chance for love and security, *bro, straight up*. If they clawed each other's eyes out, or backstabbed each other, so that one of them was left listening to Bad Bunny, in tears, while the other was contemplating therapy, so much the better.

The trick was not to care at all.

Angelica had worked very hard to have everything it took. She'd dieted down to a size two. She'd dyed her hair, been injected with the very best Botox, spray tanned and had a bio gel manicure and pedicure, had her eyebrows micro bladed, expertly applied contouring make up based on Tik Tok videos so she looked "too good to be natural."

She'd agreed to sign the pages of contracts, agreed to all the appearances on camera.

When they finally went on their date, to a restaurant in the Fontainebleau, and then dancing at LIV, all captured for the show, of course, he told her how much he liked her.

She twirled one of her dark curls around her finger, like she was flirting with him.

She put down her champagne flute. The yellow gold bubbles burned the back of her throat.

If she stayed for now at the table with him, picking at their wagyu carpaccio plate and her burrata salad, his butter soft leather loafers brushing up against her bare ankles, the white tablecloth and gardenia scented room so perfect she could laugh, her Pilates contoured abs undulating like there was nothing else she wanted more in the world than him or this.

She could be Angelica, the twenty-five-year-old receptionist, and not Cora, the almost forty-year-old sociologist under cover, who fucked a living Malibu Ken producer off camera just so she could report back. He'd had such sun kissed skin, and perfectly chiselled abs she was sure that under his pants, he'd be smooth and plastic. He had a big member, but soon admitted that he was gay.

His eyes bugged out when she suggested he call a guy he knew and make it a threesome.

"I've always wanted to be with two guys at once," she told him, and he stared at her like she'd just asked if she could give him a golden shower.

She knew it made sense. To do this kind of show, to wholeheartedly buy into this kind of fantasy, you had to be both conservative and lacking in imagination.

"This will buy me time," Ken assured her, and she felt sad for him, until he told her how much money he was making, and how relieved his parents were, which did matter to him a little.

She wondered what was in it for Golden Retriever Eyes, what he was hiding, and why he'd ever agree to this.

It surprised her, but it was fun not to be herself for a while. She could be a smoke show like that singer her colleague was researching, an ordinary face and complicated past hidden underneath piles of make up and opaque puffs of stage smoke, dancing while a celebrity she only pretended to have heard of spun music that drove the crowd around her wild.

The Best Guy I've Ever Known

He was six foot three, with eyes like twin waves at high tide, sculpted abs and sun kissed skin despite the fact that he spent all day in front of a computer, in an incredibly well-paid finance job. So if you take anything away from this, it's the shared assumption that Mark was too good for me. When you meet me, you'll see. There's nothing about me that screams extraordinary, but once we connected, Mark and I spent every free minute together.

Unlike my stay-at-home mom, construction worker dad and four siblings from a small town inexplicably named after a city in India, but pronounced Dell High, Mark just had a mother named Gemma, who had lived in twelve countries and spoke five languages. She wore silk scarves tied around her neck in a neat bow, and curly grey hair au natural. He talked to her on the phone everyday, and sometimes she asked to speak to me.

When I told people I went to art school, they either looked at me like I'd just told them I was in clown college, or they asked me to draw their portrait on the spot, like I was a cartoonist on the sidewalk with a tip cup. Mark asked me who my favourite artist was, and it wasn't like at school, where you can't say Matisse or Picasso because they're too obvious, and you can't talk about Frida Kahlo anymore than you can talk about Sylvia Plath without people rolling their eyes. Mark was curious about the arts, so I told him the truth, and he took me to the AGO on our first date. He bought me a book on Picasso that was the price of my weekly grocery bill. He said he loved how much I enjoyed being taken out, how much I loved all the bottle services and fancy dinners, sake and tuna steak, salmon tartare and cabernet sauvignon. He was great in bed, especially compared to the other guys I'd been with. I never knew if he was going to stroke my face, tell me how pretty and talented I was, then pull me on top of him, or if he was going to tie up my hands and my feet with one of his Tom Ford silk ties, yank my hair and spank me. We always said I love you during, and after.

He paid for me to join his expensive, elite gym so we could work out together. When I lost weight and started seeing some muscle, he complimented me. When I said I wanted to go blonde, and get regular manicures, he was happy to pay for it. He bought me the acrylic paint sets of my dreams, and when I told him how insecure I'd always been about my bumpy Roman nose, he paid to have it turned into a perfect, pert button, and took care of me while I recovered.

I told my best friend about him and she seemed surprised but happy for me.

The night he got caught, we were at his condo, and he said he had to run out to do a work thing. It was 11 pm, and he'd seemed antsy but it happened occasionally so I tried not to worry. He got in at 2 am, mumbling about how hard he had to work, but assuring me that he did it for us.

I was still wearing the amethyst and diamond ring he'd bought me a few weeks before when he held my hand. "Do you remember what I said about this ring?"

I nodded sleepily.

"It's a promise ring. Don't worry, the real thing will be way better. I just want you to know how much I love you."

"I know," I answered, and he fell asleep.

The next morning, the cops came in, grabbing his laptop and his phones. His eyes flashed from anger to panic and fear when they handcuffed him.

After two of them escorted him out, I stumbled over to the tall, heavy one who stood at our front door. My eyes were bleary and I could hardly get the words out.

"What is this about, anyway? What did he do?"

The cop shrugged, and then shook his head. "White collar crime, Miss. It seems he's been investing his clients' money in a Ponzi scheme. He owes millions …"

I heard myself make a retching sound. "But that can't be. He loves his job. He works so hard. His bosses love him …"

He shook his head again. "What bosses, Miss? He's the CEO, the mastermind."

I stood there in shock while he told me to take care.

Once I was sure they'd all left, I let out a huge scream.

Later that night, his mother called.

I told her that I couldn't believe it. I didn't believe he'd cheat anyone. Then she said something that made my blood go cold.

"And that woman, accusing him of sexual assault."

I thought about the Mark I knew, the generous, fun, open guy, the one who said I love you first. I needed him to be who I thought he was.

"Women don't always tell the truth." she said. "They have all kinds of motives for accusing someone."

I didn't know what to believe, my head hurt, but I knew I couldn't go back to who I was before.

"Yeah," I said, "I know. He's the best guy I've ever known."

May the Bridges You've Burned Light Your Way

I FOUND OUT ABOUT IT just like everybody else. Her social media went dark, even her *finsta,* where she posted about movies and music and occasionally books that not many people had heard of. I was always in a state of pretending with her, pretending to be cooler, pretending to care less, pretending to know what she was referencing.

She was beautiful, like an anemic Snow White, with long dark hair and Bette Davis bangs that she often cut herself, so they were charmingly uneven. She wore orange lipstick and dark liner on her full, doll like features. If she were a little taller, she would've been a famous model, but as it was, she wanted to be a musician.

She had a powerful, emotive voice, sure, with a great, expressive tone, and she wrote interesting lyrics, but more than anything, she was a star, and if you knew her, she was the whole celestial galaxy.

It's hard to explain what makes a person magnetic, why you can't take your eyes off them, why you think about what they say for hours as if there's hidden insight in every syllable, why you take their calls at all hours.

Whenever we went out to eat it was always sushi. I later learned that all that miso soup and green tea made everything come up more easily. I couldn't eat it for years after.

I had been bulimic too, when I was younger, but without much commitment. If you do bulimia really well, if you're truly committed to throwing up every single thing you've eaten, you might lose weight, I suppose. I didn't, but she was tiny, matchstick legs in skinny jeans, child-size shirts, colourful, eye grabbing style.

Her name was Alba, which was Latin for sunrise. The people closest to her called her Sunny. It took two years, including six months where we didn't talk at all, but eventually I became a member of that club. She moved to New York for an internship, and then waited tables and busked and played shows in Hell's Kitchen. She was oddly cheerful about working so hard, and always excited to hear what I was doing.

She seemed impressed with me, which was a first. In the past, she'd chided me about what she called my obsessive writing and editing. "You think work is so great," she'd said one day, "because it's more reliable than people. What you put into work, you get out, am I right? But how many relationships and friendships are you missing out on?"

Now she said she couldn't believe I'd written two books. She was excited to read them.

I became closer to a friend of hers, Chelsea, another singer she admired, whom she'd once called toxic. She begged me to visit her and to even bring Chelsea, and I said I would, but I didn't. I didn't mean to break a promise, I just didn't know how finite our time was.

I had a feeling she was lonely, even though she was always posting pictures of new friends. She wasn't writing as much or playing shows. People knew her by different names. Someone knew her as Iman. Someone else knew her as Parisa. They said she read tea leaves, that she wore smudgy black eyeliner, that her kindness was boundless. They were all in love with her. Someone graffitied her words in rainbow colours onto a Spanish Harlem Wall:

If I'm too much, go find less (I hear it's widely available)

Her sister said Sunny always hated her birthday, but that year, she let her whoop it up and serenade her, and the dread she'd had about her, her whole life, the heavy feeling, temporarily left her.

That was when it happened.

She smashed through a bedroom window, on the 24th floor of an apartment building and jumped.

I could see her, flying through the air, Manhattan panoramic and beautiful, her hair fanning out, her eyes capturing every piece of beauty like cameras.

I read about it on the internet. I had wondered where she had gone, what was happening in her life, so I googled her. I wondered if she knew how many headlines she made.

That night, I dreamed I was in the apartment with her. She was showing me a notebook full of song lyrics. "No one found the note," she said quietly, her eyes downcast.

It was one line, in her black notebook and it sounded like a song lyric.

In loving memory of when I gave a shit about what anyone like you thought

In my dream, she disappeared, and I wrote a few lines on the next page.

Dear Sunshine,
May you feel only deep happiness, and no pain
May you feel at peace with every decision you've ever made
May the bridges you've burned light your way
Into a world where you feel free, and cherished and valued
You should know that everyone here loves you and misses you,
But we all understand, like we did in life,
That stars that glisten that intensely belong to the whole universe

In my dream, she floated back for a few minutes. She read the words and nodded her head at me.

"I think you're getting better at this writing stuff," she said, and laughed.

She hugged me, and I felt her spine as my hand rested on her back.

"Promise me, you'll keep writing about everything, including me."

I nodded.

I woke up, amazed at how un-dreamlike it all felt. Later that day, I found the only photo of Sunny and me that existed. It was from when we first met, as interns at a small publishing house. We were sitting on her bed, a poster of Klimt's *The Kiss* looking down at us. We were both scribbling in our notebooks, long hair falling in front of our faces like shiny, messy curtains while PJ Harvey blared in the background. Her roommate took it.

I hope wherever she is, she's writing and singing, taking in the thrilled looks of the audience around her as she keeps creating infinitely.

Love Me Til I'm Me Again

WE USED TO DRIVE AIMLESSLY, without any destination. We'd cover bridges and ocean basins from Bedford to Dartmouth, foamy white or sea blue mansions with wraparound porches and actual white picket fences in the South End to subdivisions in Tantallon or Timberlea or Sackville, where we'd give each other bonus points if we could find a yellow door, or red paint around a window, anything that told us an individual lived here, someone weird like us, just trying, plotting their escape. There were always taller trees than I'd ever seen in Ontario, white cedars and jack pines that look like they're touching the clouds, little ponds surrounded by red oaks and black walnuts. Sometimes in my mind, I'd talk to my grandfather like he was still alive. He knew the Latin names of every tree and plant and flower that crossed our path. In my mind, we'd be walking or hiking instead of driving, and he'd examine each one with his big hands, tell me if they looked healthy, what they'd need to keep growing optimally. When he died, I walked around in a haze in Tel Aviv, not thinking or feeling much. I sat at his desk in his apartment, going through his pens and handwritten notes. I pocketed his grey luggage tag, with his name neatly spelled out then almost got run over by a car on Borgrashov street when I left. I got a tattoo, on my wrist, which I knew he'd hate, from a guy who was born in Côte D'Ivoire. It said "Tikva," which means hope in Hebrew. I got it after seeing the Know Hope graffiti tags all over the city. The pain made me feel present in my body, like I wasn't just going to float away because he was no longer there to interrogate my world views or listen to me read first drafts of my short stories.

Celi and I would breathe better when we were really far from the city. When we saw open land for miles, green field after green field, rolls of hay all pristine like a movie about idyllic rural life.

I appreciated that she never had any romantic views about farming. When your dad and grandfather are both agronomists, you grow up visiting farms the way regular families visit outlet malls. I knew more than I ever wanted to know about the optimal conditions for growing grapes versus wheat, or say, potatoes. Celi came from a place so rural she said she'd get isolation pay if she ever decided to go back and teach there.

One time we drove up to a marshy body of water, and she pulled a raft out of her trunk that she called a rubber dinghy. I was scared to get on it with her, but we didn't sink. I took off my shoes, and she put on black rubber boots, and we floated, safe as twin babies in a womb.

Celi always made me feel safe, no matter what we did. She had a soft, reassuring voice, and when she talked to her family and friends from rural Newfoundland she got extra animated. I didn't always get everything she said, between all the *yes b'ys* and *hey b'ys*, but I think I always understood the essence.

We used to call them road trips, when Celi did all of the driving and I was the world's most eager passenger. We'd stop for either Timmy's or Wendy's, the car would smell like bagels and sweet strawberry cream cheese or cheeseburgers and fries. I grew up Orthodox, and I'd been angry and rebelling against God for years, but somehow it was in Celi's car that I had my first cheeseburger, the thin patty merging with the hot slice of processed cheese, and extra ketchup I'd piled on, somehow tasting like the greatest thing I'd ever had. I remembered the exact biblical lines in Hebrew I'd learned as a kid, about not cooking a kid goat in its mother's milk, which is where the rabbis all inferred that mixing meat and dairy was wrong. I kept waiting for a thunderbolt to take me out, as if death was all I could be sure about in this life, but it never came. Celi and I ate lobster in our sushi, slurped a bowl of mussel soup at a Belgian restaurant that smelled like rotting fish, drank red and white wines and pint after pint of beer and nothing changed. I was still alive.

How do you explain wanting to get so far away from where you came from? How do you describe the restlessness, wanting to go and see and do so much that you turn your heart away from the things you're running from?

I was never in love with my ex. He had some of the right things: the long hair, the guitar playing, the love of academia. I wanted to be in love with him because, unlike my previous ex, he was ready to commit. Because he wanted to live with me right away. Because getting married was always in the cards.

I was tired of being a fuck-up, tired of turning left when everyone knew that the thing to do was turn right. So I convinced myself that the problem was me, the problem was that I wanted too much.

So he said I was fat in the beginning. Well, so did my mother. So he made me get rid of my rescue dogs. Well, my parents were happy about the improved state of my apartment. So he wanted to move to another country, and then another city, away from everyone I knew. Well, I liked adventure. So he didn't think what I was reading or listening to was all that great and substantial. Well, I was open minded. So he didn't think my writing was good enough to get published. So I wrote alone, and submitted alone and started sleeping on the hard foldout couch in our living room, because I didn't want to wake him at 3 am.

Nothing changed the fact that my marriage was over. It was like coming out of a trance I didn't know I was in. I was ashamed to tell people how badly he'd treated me, all except for Celi. She sent him the angriest text she said she'd ever sent anyone, full of more swear words and exclamation marks than she'd ever used in her life.

I told him I was going home to visit my parents and, when he said he was scared that I wasn't going to come back, knew then that I definitely wouldn't.

I spent my last night in Halifax at Celi's. We tossed and turned in the same bed, surrounded by her cats and her clothes and her comforter, and I cried because what was most irreplaceable in my life there was her, and words failed me when I tried to tell her.

The next day, on our drive to the airport, I planned an imaginary road trip to Toronto, where we'd drive to Queen St. and try to spot a white squirrel in Bellwoods, shop for hippie clothing in Kensington market, buy souvenirs and discount art supplies in Chinatown, eat *injera* and lentils and *shiro* at Sabla's restaurant on College, browse for books and graphic novels in the Annex, pick up spicy Doubles with tamarind sauce at Mona's in Scarborough, and eat them overlooking the Bluffs. There was so much I wanted her to see, so much possibility, until I thought of the perfect place. I wanted us to drive to the old Galleria mall, near Wallace Emerson park. I didn't want her to see the signs of gentrification, condos, the death of an old neighbourhood. I wanted her to see the red neon heart, the words underneath like Toronto's own Jenny Holzer installation, *Love Me Til I'm Me Again*, and I wanted her to know that she had, that she did. That she was always my touchstone.

Things that Cause Inappropriate Happiness

WE STOOD ON THE EDGE of the store, half the students edging their way into the narrow doorway. One was taking slow drags of an e-cigarette while her friend looked on, twirling a piece of hot pink hair around her finger, surreptitiously checking out three of the guys who were loitering on the sidewalk, staring at their phones, the last one, a tall, shaggy haired rock kid, with metal studs on his belt, bopping his head so hard one of his wireless headphones flew out. I bent down and handed it to him, and he nodded at me. This last store was just a bonus, and technically, I'd told them, they could go home now if they wanted to. They were well behaved, so they stayed, dragging their feet, the girls in heavy nineties redux platforms that looked better than the ones I actually wore in the nineties. So far, nothing has made me feel older than seeing clothing I wore fifteen years ago become cool again.

They weren't even really my students. My pregnant friend Tehilla, who was forced into early bed rest, convinced her principal that I'd be the perfect substitute. I was such a mediocre student, I never imagined myself standing in front of a group of kids, telling them what to do. I never imagined that they'd actually listen to me.

It was the kind of school where the kids could wear and learn whatever they wanted, so when they were into something, they were obsessed.

I didn't get obsessed with anything until I was in university. As an undergrad, I started doing large scale acrylic portraits. I used the most vibrant colours I could find, and I loved the thick, expressive textures. In studio courses, you sit with headphones on, in your own world, for hours. You forget your body. You ignore your hunger cues. You forget everything except each individual brushstroke on the page.

Tehilla was in the photography stream, but we were both obsessed with faces, with the emotions and thoughts you could discover in every line. She took pictures at my first show. It was a group show in a gallery in Parkdale, filled with women in black leather jackets, chunky highlighted hair and wing tipped eyeliner, and guys wearing T-shirts of bands I'd never heard of, bright, tribal tattoos poking out of their sleeves. I made my way towards the food, thin slices of brie and grapes, crushed Melba toast and sweaty cubes of cheddar. I had two paintings that both sold and I started to think for the first time, in a real way, that maybe I could be an artist.

When we finished school, I kept painting, working part time at a gallery and applying for grants, and she went straight into a full-time teaching job. We still saw each other, and she'd want to know all about my latest residency in Dawson City, and I'd ask to hear about her students. She'd take them to graffiti alley, or underpass park to capture all the street art on camera. They even made photography murals, and I was inspired by her energy and passion.

Getting sick happened suddenly. It started with fevers that lasted for days and wouldn't respond to Tylenol or Advil. My family doctor, Dr. Hunter, made me go to the emergency room, where they took my temperature and a bunch of tests but were puzzled too. At first, Dr. Hunter was convinced it was mono, or Epstein Barr, even when the blood tests told her otherwise. She took seventeen vials of blood one day, but she insisted that everything came back normal. I was relieved. I hoped I'd wake up one day and feel like myself again. I got red, itchy rashes on my feet and my hands, and she asked if I'd walked through poison ivy. She had me tested for allergies. She had me tested for Lyme disease, twice. My fingers hurt. They swelled so much I couldn't get my rings on. It hurt to paint.

Dr. Hunter told me about a patient with chronic fatigue syndrome who exaggerated her symptoms. Her mother told her she was so weak she couldn't even lift a spoon but when she came in for her physical, Dr. Hunter caught her lifting up her iPad. She leaned in close enough for me to smell the Dentyne Ice and lingering black coffee on her breath and said: "Don't get lazy. Push yourself all the time."

So I did. I kept sketching and painting and going to work.

My brain was foggy. I couldn't remember things, basic things I'd always known, like people's names or books I'd read or characters on TV shows. I was sure that I was going to get fired any day from the gallery.

Dr. Hunter sent me to a naturopath who was appalled that I drank Coke Zero and ate dairy.

"We have to heal your gut," Alexis said. "Lots of bone broth, greens, meat. No sugar, grains dairy and soy."

She looked me up and down. "It will also help you lose weight."

I sucked in my stomach. "Am I overweight?"

"No … but you're on the higher end of the BMI. Excess weight causes inflammation."

I couldn't shake the guilt of having done this to myself.

Every morning I woke up to the blazing, leaden weight of concrete in my fingers and toes. When I took the stairs my hips snapped, complete with cracking sounds. I couldn't do my buttons or the zippers on my jeans. Tight, hard fabrics like jeans hurt my knees, so I switched to leggings and sweats. When my feet ballooned like fiery kielbasas I went up a shoe size and half. I kept dropping things, smashing cups and plates. The lymph nodes in my neck were so swollen that when my doctor sent me for an ultrasound, I burst into tears when the technician ran over each one, one excruciating millimeter at a time.

"It's okay," she whispered. "I know I'm not supposed to tell you, but everything looks okay."

I felt both relief and frustration.

Finally, Dr. Hunter sent me to a rheumatologist. Dr. Arden pressed down on my finger joints so hard that I burst into tears. "You have rheumatoid arthritis," she said. "I don't even need to see the bloodwork." She prescribed Prednisone, and a disease-modifying-anti-rheumatic-drug called Sulfasalazine. I studied the bottles when I picked them up from the pharmacy. One of the side effects of Prednisone was inappropriate happiness.

I wondered how much happiness was appropriate now that I knew I had an incurable, chronic illness. I imagined a team of doctors, like Dr. Hunter, evaluating me, to make sure I never felt too happy. I thought about the permanent damage in my hips and my fingers. I wondered if I'd ever finish a painting again. If I'd ever do another series or if my life as an artist was over.

"Teaching is amazing," Tehilla said. "You get to talk for hours about the things you love the most, the artists, the paintings, the photos. You get to encourage and support young artists. Just try it, if you really hate it, you can quit, I'll find someone else."

So far, I'd lasted two months.

"You can go home when we're done," I promised the students, who followed me inside.

Ken, the assistant manager, who had hair dyed the colour of a goldfinch, grabbed my arm, and breathlessly pointed out a new cobalt blue they had in. "How much?" I asked, pointing to the smallest tube. "Forty-two," he said, "but probably thirty something with your discount."

My favourite kid, a fifteen-year-old named Luna, who had half shaved, half green hair, who called herself a feminist and still wore braces, came up behind me.

"Wow, good supplies are expensive."

I nodded, then headed down into the basement, where they kept their extra discounted stuff. Maybe I'd show them the slightly damaged canvases. I'd always loved stuff with character.

I turned back, but she wasn't there.

I heard the door close when I got to the bottom of the stairs.

An older man in a charcoal grey suit and a black fedora stood in the corner.

He had olive skin, a roman nose, and intense half moon shaped brown eyes framed by thick eyebrows.

"It's nice to see you, Lielle."

"How do you know my name?"

He raised an eyebrow. "I know a lot of things."

The door was closed, but the windows were open.

"You may have heard of people like me. Some of us specialize in the past. You seem to be struggling. Would you like to go back? I can take you to when you were exactly their age, to 1998."

I stared at him.

"What do you mean, take me?"

"You can sit down on this couch, right here." He held his arm out, pointing to the black leather couch beside him.

My knees burned. I sat down.

"Do I have to do anything?"

He laughed. "No. Just have a seat."

He waved his hands over me, his fingers separated like a Cohen before they start *duchening*. I wasn't religious, but I'd always found it haunting when I heard it in a synagogue on high holidays. He told me to close my eyes, and I heard him chanting the Priestly blessing in Hebrew and in English.

May God Keep you and Bless you
May His Face Shine on You and Show you Favour
May He lift His Face to You and Bring you Peace

* * *

When I open my eyes I'm lying on my stomach. I roll onto my side and feel myself falling off a bed. I jump up, suddenly realizing that I can, and that it doesn't hurt.

I stand on my tip toes. I jump up and down, lift my legs up high. I twirl like a demented ballerina until I see the clock radio on my bedside table.

6:15. Too early for anyone to be awake. My CD player stares back at me. I study the CDs on the table beside it: Tori Amos, Chumbawamba, a homemade mix which included Third Eye Blind, Aqua, Sugar Ray and Meredith Brooks, Jeff Buckley and Blur.

I notice the ceramic dollhouse shaped lamp, the books, which include *A Separate Peace*, and *Catcher in the Rye*. My desk is full of sketches of kids on skateboards and giant sunflowers, plus a half-finished math assignment. There's a full-length mirror in the closet. I stare at myself.

My light brown hair is shoulder length and thick, my skin impossibly smooth, aside from a large red pimple on my chin.

I take off my blue pajamas.

My breasts are smaller but still big enough to be a liability. I think about my cousin advising me to stock up on a bra called the minimizer, and what a waste of money it was.

I stare at my nonexistent hips. Had I had ever seen my stomach this flat?

I thought about all the cream cheese bagels and fries that I judiciously avoided, all the jeans I squeezed myself into, tearing zippers into my skin, thinking I deserved it because they were too tight.

I look at my lean fingers, press down on my joints, and there's no excess synovial fluid, no pain. I edge over to my childish jewellery box. It has a broken ballerina but still plays a song from *Beauty and the Beast*. I pull out all my rings, the enamel daisy that was my mom's, the gold ruby heart from my grandmother, the silver flower. I put them all on, wiggling my fingers, shaking my wrists. I clap like a two-year-old, and it doesn't hurt. I want to wake everyone so I can high five them.

I remember the code to our family's alarm, it's never changed and I leave a note telling them I've gone for a run.

I run and I run, the wind blowing through my hair and I push and my muscles hurt in the best way but my joints feel nothing, my knees feel nothing as I pound the concrete, my body feels paper light, and I run block after block after block.

I get back and get dressed, in jeans that are massive and wide and floor sweeping.

My mom offers to drive me to school. She thinks it's weird that I hug her for so long, and that I'm so excited to eat the scrambled eggs and toast she's made me.

The first person I see at school is Samantha.

She's wearing a purple velour tank top, the straps carefully hidden under a light jean button down shirt, and flares. Her brown hair is stick straight. I get closer and smooth out a piece in the back. She jumps and turns around, then laughs when she realizes it's me. She has huge brown eyes and a sweet smile. I want to tell her how beautiful she is.

I think of how adrift I'll be when we stop being friends. I think about her need to be the best at everything, starting with her grades. I think of how she'll abandon me when I get involved with a guy who treats me badly, how she'll criticize me for not having more self control, and when my grades slip she'll say, "I told you."

I think of how bright her future will be: at first, a full scholarship to the best university, a boyfriend who'll become a fiancée whom she'll travel the world with, an impressive job, and a beautiful wedding on a golf course. And then she'll die not long afterwards. It'll have been so long that, when I hear the news, months later, I won't even be able to call her parents.

"What?" she says eventually. "You're like, staring at me." I look down at the huge pink Baby G watch on my wrist, wishing it was an Apple watch.

"I dunno," I say. "Can I call you right after school? "

She nods, gum popping. I reach over and hug her. She smells like the floral, plastic-y smell of Gap's Dream and Woolite.

"You know what, can you call after *Dawson's Creek*? Anytime after 9 is good."

I somehow know that it will be too late by then, and a sadness hits me.

"I'm really happy that we're friends, Sami. I think you're awesome. Can we try harder to support each other?"

She nods again, her eyes enormous. "Whatever you say, weirdo."

I see Tehilla on my way to my next class. She's wearing her usual form-hiding black sweats, loose black T-shirt and her hair in a high, messy bun, her face beaming. The sight is so comforting I give her a hug.

"Lee. It's good to see you too." Tehilla has always been more adult than a kid. She was the kind of girl teachers always used as their example.

I ask her if she wants to have lunch together, and she nods.

She picks at a sandwich; I eat another apple.

"You need to eat more carbs," she says, and I ask her if she has a Toonie. We split a giant chocolate chip cookie from the cafeteria, and we laugh.

"Hey, Tehilla." I turn to her, suddenly serious. "How do you know you want to be a photographer?"

"I just really love taking photos. I could spend hours reading about it and trying different settings. Isn't that how you feel about painting?"

"I think so. But can I ask you something? What would you do if you couldn't take photos anymore? If you got sick, or if you were in an accident and you hurt your hands?"

"I think," she says eventually, "that I'd probably find a way to keep doing it. Maybe I'd have to go slow, only take one photo a day. Maybe I'd find a job that's related to it, like ..." She pauses. "I don't know, graphic design. Maybe I'd work in a gallery."

I laugh. I think about her as an adult, how she'd spent years casually dating until she met Emma. I think about their son, and the baby to come, how they both took turns being pregnant. Their life is so perfect and full.

She leans in. "I think I'd be depressed if it got too hard for me to take photos. I wouldn't know who I was anymore."

I reach for her, until I feel a hand on my shoulder.

I hear chanting, and I open my eyes to find myself back in the basement.

He helps me to my feet.

"So," he says, his expression somewhere between a smile and a grimace. "How do you feel?"

I try to articulate all the feelings I've had, and I find myself laughing.

"Sadness. Nostalgia. Love. Inappropriate happiness. Did anyone ever tell you," I start to ask him, "that you look just like ...?"

"I know," he said, cutting me off. "But you have to know your audience. You're an artist, Lielle. I had to take on the image of the Cohen you most admire. Or at least one you'd actually recognize. His Hebrew name was Eliezer."

He laughs, and I hear him sing a line from "Hallelujah," the one about all he ever learned from love, before he disappears.

I feel hot tears running down my face, but I start to smile as I make my way slowly up the stairs.

There's Something I've Been Meaning to Say to You

"Then her friend chimed in saying get a clue/
Get a life, put it in your song/
There's something I've been meaning to say to you ..."
—Brendan Benson, Metarie

I WROTE MY FIRST MESSAGE and displayed it in my kitchen window, which anyone passing my ground floor apartment could see easily. It was a long sign, in black pen, in my sloping handwritten script, and it was a huge contrast to all the people who'd colourfully thanked first responders in the first wave and never bothered to take their signs down.

There's something I've been meaning to say to you. Sometimes I miss the things we used to do together. Going to farmers' markets full of local craftspeople selling overpriced infinity scarves and handmade moisturizer made in someone's bathroom that smelled vaguely of lemongrass and lavender, that you insisted on buying for me. I miss the vegan organic restaurants you'd drag me to that I thought would be terrible, but often weren't. I miss you taking me for walks on Woodbine beach, where that's

all we did. I miss you taking me to Fringe festival plays that I didn't think were funny, or music showcases where you complained that the guitarist's E string was flat, and I nodded like I understood what you meant. I miss watching you eat deep fried shrimp and fries while you never gained a pound. I miss going to Kensington and spending our last five dollars and change for something we'd never end up wearing from *Courage My Love*. I miss secretly reading your diary, where you were freer and more confident than you ever were in real life. I miss watching you show off gold jewellery your boyfriend bought you, so proud I'd almost forget that he'd cheated on you.

At first no one said anything about the sign, but then neighbours I'd never properly met, people who lived in the building or even in some of the nearby houses, people whose names I'd never learned even after six years of living here, started talking to me. It had always been weird to rent an apartment in one of the two low rise buildings in a sea of very expensive houses and condo units. It was a safe neighborhood, with beautiful ravines, and green spaces, where everyone was polite but I still didn't have a single friend.

Suddenly people started telling me about their break ups, and we'd stand on the sidewalk outside my building, smoking or drinking cold coffee, exchanging stories about our lives. Maybe the pandemic had made us all lonelier, and more eager to share. Maybe we were all thinking too much, desperate to share our new epiphanies.

I decided to keep going. I went to the dollar store and got two boxes of the thinnest sidewalk chalk I could find. I went out into the back parking lot after midnight, using the flashlight on my phone. I wrote all over every empty parking spot. Some were immediately smudged and erased when cars were parked in them, others were judiciously avoided.

There's something I've been meaning to say to you. I'll never forgive you for the way you dropped me. I'd worked so hard to be a presence in your life and boy, did you make me earn it. Your childhood traumas don't justify your behaviour. Lots of people have shitty parents or get bullied; some people learn that in life there's only an aggressor and a victim, and nothing in between. I wish it had made you more self-aware and more empathetic. There's a great scene about this in *A Tree Grows in Brooklyn.* I wish we were still friends so we could still talk about books. I miss the way you analyzed movies. I loved the *Virgin Suicides* until you said it seemed like Coppola had a girl crush on Kristen Dunst; the book had so much more depth, you argued. Remember when we were fifteen, and we went to see the movie *Titanic* at the movie theatre in Yorkdale? Neither of us liked it. We were like two pop culture voyeurs, watching something teenagers were supposed to like, just to say we actually did it. Remember when we were thirteen, and you said it was embarrassing that I liked the Spice Girls, and then you explained to me what a prefabricated group was? Remember when we were seventeen, driving around in your car, listening to the Doors? Blasting Jim Morrison's lyrics embarrassed me.

I walked around the neighbourhood and noticed all the signs on telephone poles, for dog walkers and babysitting and window cleaning and housekeeping. I envied people who could still work, while I sat inside, immunocompromised from the biologics I had to insert into my arm once a week with a spring-loaded needle. While I waited for my next vaccine, I read online about autoimmune conditions like mine, Ankylosing Spondylitis and COVID and why people thought if something happened to me, it would be because of my "pre-existing condition." I read about people's resentment that they had to keep thinking about people who were probably just going to die anyway.

I scribbled on a blank piece of paper and borrowed a heavy duty stapler from Amy in the apartment next door.

There's something I've been meaning to say to you. When we were friends, I was the definition of insane, trying so hard, again and again hoping things would be different. I blocked you on one social media platform; you blocked me on two others. I didn't think you still thought about me, but I bumped into a former friend of yours and she said you talked about me all the time. She said you were obsessed with my career. She also called you a narcissist and something in me released. I stopped focusing on lies I knew I'd told you, on the stupid ways I'd created to save face around you because you made me feel so inadequate. I didn't know how different we were. It was okay for you to have a persona, to exaggerate your successes, to inflate yourself so your achievements hung over everyone like the shadow of a punctured balloon, but it wasn't okay for anyone else.

There's something I've been meaning to say to you. When we had coffee in that café on Roncesvalles, a flourish of your stiff, blazer jacketed arms, a sweep of your impossibly long legs when you offered to pay for me, but were

forty minutes late. All I cost you was five dollars and twelve cents. All I could think about was the time we met at your house in the Annex where you were moving, years earlier. I didn't see your offhand callousness coming. After that, If I saw you around, you were friendly, but pretended not to really remember me. Then you acted like I mattered, again if only briefly. When you grilled me about my past, you forgot to ask me one important question: what I learned from it. Here's the answer you wouldn't have wanted to hear: I learned not to trust people like you.

On one of my walks I passed a wet, newly paved sidewalk. I grabbed a stick and before anyone noticed I carved in "There's something I've been meaning to say to you." When you find a way to contradict me, when you try to poke a hole in my perception, it makes me pity you. I waited for someone to complain or someone to call the city, but no one did.

A week later, there were three little kids who'd set up a lemonade stand two houses down from my apartment. Summer was over, so it was a little weird, but the schools were still closed and I guess the kids were bored. I bought a cup, and a chocolate chip cookie, and kept walking. They left the stand out over overnight, so they were set up for the next day. That night I scribbled something down on a small piece of notebook paper and taped it to the side.

There's something I've been meaning to say to you, my goals are meaningful to me. I don't like to talk about them, I prefer to just get them done.

For Halloween, none of the kids were allowed to trick or treat, but all the houses decorated their lawns with gravestones and skeletons. My favourite was the giant house on the corner, with a gravestone that said: *I did my own research*.

I bought a smaller, pale beige gravestone decoration from the Dollar store down the street, wrote on it with a thick, black Sharpie, then snuck onto their lawn, and put it right beside it.

There's something I've meaning to say to you. I see your out of control, unmedicated anxiety. You probably can't see my autoimmune disorder. I go to great lengths to hide it. Stop treating me, and people like me like our lives our disposable, like we're weak, like we did something wrong because what we want is to continue to exist.

I didn't know if I had gone too far, if people had started to get angry, if I'd gotten too intensely into all of this. I was having dreams about becoming a graffiti artist, writing sentences on bridges and freeways.

I decided to do one more. I cut a piece of blank paper into a small heart, like the glowing neon heart lights I'd seen in windows all over the city. I wrote on it and put it in the corner of my bedroom window, where anyone who passed the building could see it.

There's something I've been meaning to say to you. I cried when people criticized my work in the past, but I cried more thinking about you not bothering to think about it or read it. All I wanted was for you to see me.

Acknowledgements

Enormous thanks to Michael Mirolla, who believed in this collection, and was so supportive, and helpful and a wonderful editor to work with. Enormous thanks also to Anna van Valkenburg, who is always a joy to be around, and the rest of the wonderful Guernica Editions team. It's been a dream getting to work with all of you.

Thank you so much to Rafael Chimicatti, for the cover design genius, and the enthusiasm. It was a joy to work with you.

Thank you so much to the lovely editors who chose some of these stories for their publications, and believed in them in their earlier, messier forms.

Thank you to the wonderful Dane Swan, who chose "Sometimes I Like to Shoot Kids" for his anthology *Changing the Face of Canadian Literature*.

Thank you to Sarah Feldbloom for choosing "Aloha State" for the *Humber Literary Review*.

Thank you to Nora Gold for choosing "Don't Look Back" for *Jewishfiction.net*.

Thank you to Emily Perkovich from Querencia Press, for choosing "Born, Not Made" for their Winter 2023 Anthology.

Thank you to Kristen Henderson for choosing "The Name Game" for *Bright Flash Literary Review*.

Thank you to Gal Slonim for choosing "Able to Pass" for the *Beyond Words Literary Review*. Thank you for your invaluable insights, and the time you took to share them. The ending is so much better because of you.

Thank you to Suzanne Craig-Whytock for choosing "Together We Stand" for *Dark Winter Literary Magazine*, and for being so lovely to work with.

Thank you to Anthony Emerson and the lovely team at *Assignment Magazine* for choosing "Soulmates".

Thank you so much to Zoe Moldenhauer at *The Aerogramme Center's Mobile Literary Magazine* for choosing "Things That Cause Inappropriate Happiness" for their Young Adult/Capsule issue.

Thank you to Alanna Rusnak for choosing "Things that Cause Inappropriate Happiness" for the Dec 2023 issue of *Blank Spaces Magazine*, for sharing the love of Leonard Cohen, and for understanding everything so deeply.

Thank you to Leah Eichler for choosing "Rats in Disguise" for *Esoterica Magazine*, for the amazing edits, and equally wonderful conversations about writing and art.

Thank you to the editorial staff of *On the Run Magazine* for choosing "The Best Guy I've Ever Known".

Thank you to Mari-Lou Rowley at *Grain Magazine* for choosing "Dark and Lilac Fairies" for their 50th anniversary issue. It's such an honour to be included.

Thanks to Michelle Richmond at *Hidden Attic Press* for reprinting "Dark and Lilac Fairies" and for all of your enthusiasm and support.

Thank you to Ashton and the rest of the editorial team at *Moot Point Magazine* for choosing "If You're Not Careful, You'll Be Lonely".

Thank you to Martin Chipperfield at 34th *Parallel Magazine* for so quickly and enthusiastically choosing "All the Lives that Could Have Been".

Thank you to John Bowie at *Bristol Noir* for choosing "Blasting Molly Rockets," and "May the Bridges You've Burned Light Your Way," for giving such generous, thoughtful feedback.

Thanks to the lovely team at *Berlin Literary Review* for choosing "Happiness Contained in A Single Bite," and for all the kind words.

Thank you to Shane Neilson for choosing "There's Something I've Been Meaning to Say to You" for *Hamilton Arts and Letters*.

Thank you to Garrett Souliere at *Quibble Literary Review* for choosing "Look at Him," and thank you for pairing it with Tara Thiel's beautiful art. It was an honour all around.

Thank you so much to the editors at *Fauxmoir* for choosing "A Good Story to Tell" and for being so excited about it.

Thank you to Genna Rivieccio from *The Opiate Magazine* for choosing both "Like An Alligator Eyeing a Small Fish" and "Black Market Encounters" Thank you so much for your support.

Thank you to Kate Geiselman at *Flights Magazine* for choosing "From the Belly of the Whale," and for your kind words about the story.

Thank you to Cary Fagan, Rebecca Comay and Bernard Kelly for choosing "Always An Angel, Never A God, for *Espresso Chapbooks* short story series, and for their insight and support

Thank you to Stephen J Golds at *Punk Noir Magazine* for choosing "Always An Angel, Never A God," and for the enthusiasm and support.

Thank you to Darcie Friessen Hossack for choosing "There's Something I've Been Meaning to Say to You" for *Word City Literary Magazine*, and for their wonderful support.

Thank you to Shane Neilson for choosing the longer version of this story for *Hamilton Arts and Letters*.

Thank you to Emily Makere Broadmore and the rest of the amazing *Folly Journal* team, for choosing "Smoke Show" for the short list of their International Short story competition. I'm thrilled to imagine my stories making it all the way to New Zealand!

Thank you to Clarissa Hurley for choosing "Proteksiye and Mazel" for *Camel Magazine*, and for the wonderful, thoughtful edits.

Thank you to Kevin Watson of *Prime Numbers Magazine/Press* 53 for choosing an early version of "Love Me Til I'm Me Again" (called "Last Night in Halifax") as the second place winner for their International Flash Fiction Prize.

Thank you to Alison Smith of the *Lincoln Review* for choosing "When You Play with Fire." So grateful for your support.

Thank you so much to Douglas Smith of *The Antigonish Review* for choosing "Love Me Til I'm Me Again" for TAR issue 214. It's an honour.

Thank you so much to the amazing Carleigh Baker, Gary Barwin, Kathy Friedman, Leesa Dean, Sidura Ludwig and JJ Dupuis for the generous blurbs and for the support.

Thank you to Carleigh for the amazing notes on "There's Something I've Been Meaning to Say to You," and for the support and friendship.

Thank you to Elee Kraljii Gardiner for her support of my art and my Canadian Author Series.

For friendship and community and so many years of support and literary adventures all my thanks to Heather Wood and Shirarose Wilensky. I'm so lucky to have you both in my life. Special thanks to Shirarose for the incredibly thoughtful early notes, and to Heather, whose enthusiasm, talent, reliability and big heart has powered my writing since the early days of your writing group at U of T. I love you both.

I was so lucky to do my MFA at Guelph, in such a supportive and community-based environment. My eternal gratitude to Catherine Bush, Dionne Brand and Michael Winter, and to my incredibly talented classmates, who included Chris Bailey, Rebecca Love, Nadine Sander-Green, Sarah Feldbloom, Adnan Khan, Jessica Popeski, Julie Mannell, Aaron Tang, Ana Machado, David Bradford, Lindsay Miles, Jacquie Zong-Li Ross, Simone Dalton, Owain Nicholson and Cassandra Williamson-Hopp.

Thank you so much to my writing students who inspire me every day. It's an honour to get to work with you. Thank you for trusting me with your stories.

Thank you so much to Alissa York, Richard Scrimger and David Bezmosgis for being a dream to work for, for advice and thoughts and wonderful conversations that I value so much.

Thank you to Lee Gowan and Emily Sandford.

Thank you to the women of the Heliconian Club's literature section. I was so honoured to be your writer in residence, and I'm honoured to be part of your beautiful community.

Thank you to the writing community, whose work I admire so much and whose kindness I always aspire to reciprocate and then some. Special thanks to Elyse Friedman, Leesa Dean, Kamal Al Solaylee, Grace O'Connell, Zoe Whittall, Emily Schultz, Lynn Crosbie, Ayelet Tsabari, Kathy Friedman, Kevin Hardcastle, Adam Sol, Chris Bailey, Brent Van Staalduinen, Dina Del Bucchia, Carleigh Baker, Jen Sook Fong Lee, Catherine Black, Stephanie Wyled, Nora Gold, Ann Choi, Kelly S Thompson, Samantha Bailey and Carrianne Leung.

Thank you to all the people who've expressed enthusiasm for this and other projects, including Ben McNally (and of course, Danielle and Rupert), Alison Gadsby at Junction Reads, Rabbi Adam Cutler for being the best host, and for inviting me to talk about books, and all the stores, reading series' and festivals that have been kind enough to host me. Doing book tours is a dream come true.

Thank you to my amazing family, my incredible, supportive husband Micah Vernon, who patiently read every draft and offered thoughts on everything, who let me talk at length about sentences and paragraphs and characters or sit contemplating things mid draft. You're the best partner anyone could ask for, and I'm grateful everyday that you chose me. Our amazing kids, Lev and Zohar, who bring so much light and love, and hilarious questions and observations. Our pups, C and N (who patiently sit while I read paragraphs out loud, moving their heads side to side, trying to understand) my parents, Nurit and Martin, who also read many drafts and encouraged me when I wanted to put my head through my computer screen, my brothers, Ari and Yoel, my sister-in-law Brooke and niece Fleur for being the best. My amazing friends, Yael, Michelle, Kate, Lara, Leanne, Ariella and Bronwyn, for always being there (and for letting me borrow your generous hearts, interests and turns of phrase for so many years).

Thank you, most of all, for reading these stories.

About the Author

Danila Botha is the author of three short story collections, *Got No Secrets, For All the Men (and Some of the Women) I've Known*, which was a finalist for the Trillium Book Award, The Vine Awards and the ReLit Award, and *Things that Cause Inappropriate Happiness*. She is also the author of the award winning novel *Much on the Inside* which was recently optioned for film. Her new novel, *A Place for People Like Us* will be published by Guernica Editions in 2025. She is part of the faculty at Humber School for Writers, and she teaches Creative Writing at University of Toronto's School of Continuing Studies. She lives in Toronto with her family.

Printed by Imprimerie Gauvin
Gatineau, Québec